SHOW ME
THE EVIDENCE

SHOW ME THE EVIDENCE

Alane Ferguson

Bradbury Press New York

Bradbury Press
An Affiliate of Macmillan, Inc.
866 Third Avenue, New York, NY 10022
Collier Macmillan Canada, Inc.
Printed and bound in the United States of America First Edition
10 9 8 7 6 5 4 3 2 1

The text of this book is set in 12 point Times Roman.
Book design by Julie Quan

LIBRARY OF CONGRESS CATALOGING-IN-PUBLICATION DATA
Ferguson, Alane.
Show me the evidence / Alane Ferguson.
p.   cm.
Summary: When, after a bizarre series of events, her
best friend is accused of murdering her own baby brother
and two other babies, Lauren, convinced of her friend's
innocence, joins her in trying to solve the mystery and
find evidence to clear her name.
ISBN 0-02-734521-1
[1. Mystery and detective stories.   2. Kidnapping—Fiction.
3. Baby sitters—Fiction.]   I. Title.
PZ7.F3547Sh   1989
[Fic]—dc19   88-39203   CIP   AC

This novel is a work of fiction. Names, characters, places, and incidents are either the product of the author's imagination or are used fictitiously. Any resemblance to actual events or persons, living or dead, is entirely coincidental.

For Margarett and Jerold Ferguson,
who gave me my greatest gift—their son.

1

Lauren leaned against her locker and waited for Janaan, enjoying the coolness of metal against her damp back. All around her, locker doors slammed with machine-gun echoes as students milled out the heavy glass doors, then scattered like blown leaves. It was hot and stuffy in the hallway. It was four o'clock. Those two reasons alone made Lauren anxious to escape into the fresh air outside. But she didn't want to, couldn't take the chance of missing Janaan, not after what she'd found hidden in the bottom of their locker.

Her mind tumbled with thoughts of Janaan, her very best friend, who shared every secret Lauren had. Sharp and funny, Janaan was the type of girl from whom problems slid the way water slips around a stone. Lauren had known her for years—or had she? The thought of what she'd found, now discreetly tucked in her purse, made Lauren's stomach turn. Just keep it light until we're in the car, she told herself for the tenth time. Then we can talk. She scanned the crowd of faces until she spotted her friend making her way through the hall. Janaan was small and exotic, with luscious hair so dark it seemed woven with strands of blue. She moved with a sleek elegance Lauren envied, and her large, green-flecked eyes tilted up at the corners, like a cat's. Nothing escaped those eyes. Ever.

"Scoot over so I can unload these," Janaan said, lightly tapping Lauren's hip. "Can you believe this heat? I think I lost five pounds to dehydration, which is the only good thing I can say about it. I knew I'd hate having phys ed at the end of the day."

She shoved a mound of dog-eared books into the bottom shelf, then flashed a smile at Lauren.

"You look disgustingly cool. I want to know why blonds don't sweat."

"You obviously haven't been in smelling distance of Larry Speck," Lauren shot back, wrinkling her nose. "I just came from a hot room with him and I almost sprayed disinfectant on his smelly little body."

Janaan laughed and eyed her reflection in the mirror that hung inside their locker door. Her almond-shaped eyes looked shadowed, at odds with her bright chatter. Lauren wasn't fooled by that carefree attitude, not now. Why hadn't she noticed something sooner?

"Just one more pebble to add to the I'd-rather-be-blond pile." Janaan sighed, combing her fingers through her damp hair.

She grabbed a blue folder, then fell into step with Lauren as they had almost every day for the past four years. The crowd of students had thinned, exposing a flurry of crumpled paper scattered across the hallway.

With less than three weeks of the school year left, lockers everywhere were being purged of eight months of garbage. If only Janaan had cleaned out her things yesterday, Lauren thought. She wished she hadn't made the discovery.

Say something, Lauren commanded herself. "How did it go with Steven today? Did you make contact? Only fifteen shopping days left until school's out for the summer."

Janaan fished around in her purse as they walked. "Aha, here it is, my last piece of gum, which I will generously split with you. As far as the plan to get Steven to ask me out—it was a bust. I didn't even try."

"Why not? Your dad hasn't . . ."

Quickly shaking her head, Janaan said, "No, he hasn't figured anything out yet—he still thinks I've given in to his stupid demands. As far as he knows, I don't date. Period. It was just . . . since he's going out of town . . . oh well, *c'est la vie.*"

Lauren kicked a crushed 7 Up can out of her path and asked, "So why didn't you try for Steven?"

"Why bother? I heard Cynthia Walker talking in the lav. *She's* been dating Steve, lucky fellow, and their last date sounded like a real steamy one. After Cynthia, I would definitely be anticlimactic, pardon the pun."

"That Cynthia is as discriminating as a dog in heat." Lauren sniffed. She reached over to give Janaan's thin shoulder a squeeze. "Take comfort in the fact that they're both dating beneath themselves."

Janaan smiled, then shrugged. "Anyway, if you really want to help me out of my post-Steven depression, how about shopping with me tomorrow at the mall? PCCIH—Parental Credit Card In Hand. Would ten o'clock be okay?"

"I'm baby-sitting. Mrs. Bloom must have a spy—she always calls when we have a day off for parent-teacher conferences. Maybe after, okay?"

They heaved open the doors and stepped into intense heat. The sky was endless blue, streaked with an occasional cloud that looked like cotton stretched too thin. It was laying-out weather. Lauren's complexion was as pale as her hair, and she was desperate to get some color on her legs. Until she baked herself from white to at least a beige, she refused to wear shorts next to Janaan, who was half Arab and perpetually tan.

Crossing the parking lot, they reached Lauren's car, an old blue Pinto she'd inherited from her brother Mark.

Cautious, trying to keep any bare skin from touching the hot vinyl, they eased themselves into the grayed bucket seats. The inside air was stifling. Her car seemed to shudder as Lauren inched into the stream of students flowing out of Skyline's parking lot.

"You know, I hate to say this, but I'm kinda glad it didn't work out with Steve. I mean, aren't you scared of getting caught dating behind your dad's back? Every time you try for a guy, I get nightmares. What would your dad do if he ever found out?"

"He'd kill me very slowly, then boil my date. No big deal."

"I'm not kidding, Janny. Why don't you just wait a few more months? You'll be in college. He can't stop you then."

"Uh-huh. Spoken like someone who can date any time she feels like it. You know how long it's been since he made that stupid rule? Six months!"

"Ever since . . . ?"

"Yes. Ever since Adam," Janaan answered impatiently. "Let's talk about something else."

"Oh. Okay." Lauren hesitated, searching for the right words, the right tone, then plunged ahead.

"Now don't get mad, but as long as we're changing the subject, I wanted to ask you about something I found in our locker today."

Lauren sensed, more than saw, Janaan stiffen. "There are lots of things in our locker, including an apple core you left there from lunch. Can you be a little more specific?" Her voice was cold.

Lauren stole a glance at Janaan. She was leaning against the door, intently twisting a cubic zirconia ring around her middle finger. Her hair hung into her face, hiding her features, making them impossible to read.

"I mean the picture."

There was a long pause. Lauren was glad she was driving, because it gave her something to concentrate on while she waited for Janaan to talk to her, to explain.

"What were you doing in my things!"

"I wasn't in your things. I was just searching for my calculus assignment."

"Under *my* books. Right. That's like looking in *my* wallet for *your* money."

Lauren willed herself to be patient. "Okay, I'm sorry. But Janaan, I gave you that picture. It was your birthday present. How could you?"

"How could I what? I was having a bad day, okay? Give me the negative and I'll get another one made. Will that satisfy you?" Janaan spat out the words. "It better, because I don't *owe* you anything, particularly an explanation of what I do or why I do it! And from now on, you'd better stay out of my things!"

Lauren wasn't prepared for the venom in Janaan's voice. She felt her face get hot, could feel color blotching down her neck. It had gone all wrong. She had planned that she and Janaan would talk openly the way they always had, and Janaan would tell her why she had mauled her birthday gift, a photograph of the two of them taken last summer.

It was a picture Lauren's mother had snapped when they were at the beach, both in bikinis, Janaan with a Garfield and Lauren with an Odie towel wrapped tightly around their middles. Lauren's arm was draped across Janaan's back, and Janaan's head was tilted to one side, her mouth open wide because Lauren's mother had caught her laughing. Lauren loved that picture. Except that it no longer looked the way it had. When Lauren found the picture it was out of its frame, crumpled and dirty, with Janaan's face erased, so that only a white circle remained. Her shoulders and breasts were partially gone, smudged into nothingness. Lauren's face hadn't been erased, but a gouge ran from her temple to the middle of her chest.

At first she'd been startled, then angry, then frightened. What was Janaan thinking of? Why would she destroy the reminder of a great day?

This person huddled against the door of her car seemed a stranger. The silence hung heavy between them, each minute taunting Lauren to say something that would break it. Janaan stared stiffly out the passenger window, twisted away from Lauren, dismissing her. They were already winding down Janaan's street, a lazy asphalt ribbon lined with ancient trees that wove their branches into gnarled arches. If she were going to say something, she'd have to do it now.

"Janaan?" Lauren began, her voice almost a whisper. "I'm not mad about the picture. I mean, I'm not mad that you messed it up. The only reason I said anything is because if there's something wrong, I want to know about it." She took a deep breath, then turned to see Janaan's face. All she saw was the back of her head.

"Say something. Anything."

Janaan didn't move.

"Did I do something wrong . . . ?"

Finally Janaan turned toward Lauren, her face pained and drawn. "It's not you, Laurie. I don't know why I did it. Please don't read any deep psychological meaning into that picture, okay? Please? Haven't you ever done anything stupid? Dumb question, of course not. Perfect Laurie, with her perfect parents in her perfect house."

Lauren had pulled into Janaan's driveway, close to the flat, sprawling rambler overhung with weeping trees. From the outside, Janaan's home looked deceptively small, but inside, the rooms connected into each other like a maze. Lauren stared at the newly blooming marigolds that erupted along the walkway, the only splashes of color amid the massive tangle of green.

"I'm sorry," Janaan whispered. "I don't know what's wrong with me lately."

"It's all right," Lauren answered quietly. Maybe she was overreacting. At that moment all she felt was tired, tired of verbal dueling when she was only trying to help, tired of Janaan. Maybe it wasn't any of her business, anyway. She just wanted to go home.

"I know I'm a pain," Janaan said. "Only you would put up with me."

Lauren didn't answer. A bee bounced across the windshield, then crawled slowly along the wiper blade. Lauren could hear Janaan shift in her seat, but concentrated on the delicate bee legs as they groped across the chrome shaft. Janaan's voice, hanging somewhere between a murmur and a whisper, broke again into the silence.

"You're right, Laurie, we do need to talk. How about tomorrow? Could I—do you think I could sit with you at the Blooms?"

"I don't think they'd mind," Lauren said deliberately, "but I know how you feel about sitting ever since Adam . . ."

"No, that's fine. If you can do it, I can, too." She squeezed Lauren's hand long and hard, then opened the car door and slid out into her driveway.

"See you tomorrow."

Janaan disappeared into the wild greenery that crowded the entryway to her home.

2

A noise worked its way into Lauren's groggy mind, penetrating her sleep, intruding into her dream, until she gave up and opened her eyes. A broken sprinkler head sputtered and hissed directly under her window. She focused on her alarm clock as the large digital numbers slipped silently into place. It was 7:32. Wrapping her pillow around her head, she squeezed her eyes shut and tried to catch the dream that slipped along the corners of her memory.

It was something about Janaan, something faintly disturbing. But the vapors were gone, thinned into wisps that dissolved into nothing.

She yawned and stretched her arms above her head, flexing the blood into her fingers and toes. The outer edges of her sheets felt cool, chilling her.

Janaan. The photograph crystallized in her mind. Something was wrong, but what? Ever since Adam died, Janaan had been guarded, almost secretive, shutting Lauren out from her innermost feelings. It was so different from the way things used to be. They'd always been able to talk about anything. Now Janaan would open only so far, and then a hidden latch would spring, and a door inside would slam shut.

Lauren's thoughts drifted to the last time Janaan had slept over. The two of them had nestled into sleeping bags, with a huge bowl of chips and a bigger bowl of popcorn between them.

"Why is it we never get any dates with the A list?" Lauren had asked, munching a Frito. "What do you think, does Cynthia really have the secret to dating success?"

"You mean falling into bed with every guy she goes out with? I hardly think so. Have you noticed she never looks very happy?"

"Well, Cynthia may not, but her boyfriends always do." Lauren giggled. "Seriously though, when do you think you'll take the plunge? I mean, we always say we'll get married first."

"You and me? Married? I think my mother wants a son-in-law."

"Very funny. You know what I meant. *The act.* Don't you ever wonder what it will be like?"

Janaan had rolled onto her back. Her dark hair fanned the carpet, creating a silky halo around her face as her gaze wandered the ceiling. "I haven't met a guy yet that's worth having sex with, Laurie, and when I do, he'll be the one I'll want to marry, so I'll marry him and it'll all work out."

"I know. That's the way I've got it planned, too. It's just . . . aren't you . . . curious?"

"Nope. From what I've seen, I just wonder if I'll even get married at all." She pulled a strand of hair, then began to twist it. "The way I figure, most guys are users. My dad uses my mother all the time. Cynthia's groupies use her. So why get married and give some guy legal rights over me? I'm already controlled enough."

Lauren had leaned over to punch her arm. "Come on, Janny. Guys aren't so bad. You're turning into a genuine pessimist."

"No I'm not. I'm just turning smart." She'd twisted the hair tighter. "I know how screwed up life can get, and I don't believe 'everything always works out in the end' anymore." Her eyes, as they stared past Lauren, had been distant, clouded. "You know what, Laurie? Sometimes I feel like I'm a lot older than my age. And sometimes . . . I think . . ." Her voice trailed.

Lauren waited, but the moment died as quickly as it had begun.

"Gawd, forget this!" Janaan released the coil of hair and scrambled to her feet. "I can get depressed at home. We need music, something loud. I'll go through Mark's old stash of tapes. Be right back."

Lauren hadn't pressed. The truth was, Janaan was more fun when she was *up,* and it was easier to let her bad moods slide. Now, lying in bed while the sprinkler sputtered outside, Lauren worried again about the photograph. She wished she'd tried harder to get inside Janaan's mind. Sighing, she groped on the floor for her slippers. Whatever was bothering Janaan would have to be dealt with later. Right now she was hungry.

After sliding out of bed she made her way to her bathroom, splashed cold water on her face, and grabbed a towel. Her period was about to start and she was puffy, especially around the eyes. As she blotted her skin she found a new pimple near her hairline, fingered it in disgust, then tousled her bangs to cover it. She wore her thick, sand-gold hair to the middle of her back, with sun-bleached bangs feathered to her dark brows. High cheekbones, a gift of Swedish ancestors, curved beneath her large, aquamarine eyes. They were ringed in deeper blue, just like her father's, and her nose was a smaller, more upturned version of his. That suited her, but her large mouth was her mother's, and Lauren hated it. She turned sideways to study her reflection, smoothing her nightgown over her stomach. You're fat, she told herself. You're fat and your skin's breaking out—what a mess!

A knock sounded softly on her door. "Are you dressed yet, Laurie?" her mother asked. "Breakfast is made if you want some."

"I'll be right down!" Lauren called through her door. Moments later she clattered down the stairs to the kitchen.

"How about some French toast and bacon?" her mother asked after Lauren had settled into the bench that curved along the bay window.

"French toast sounds great, but forget the bacon," Lauren answered, yawning. "Bacon is full of fat—just like me."

Her mother chose to ignore that. "Want a cup of coffee?" she asked.

"Sure."

Lauren rested her chin in her hand and watched her mother. Although Marilyn Taylor was nearing fifty, she wore her graying hair to her shoulders, blunt and unstyled. While other women her age wore designer labels, Marilyn taught in jeans and oversized shirts, her reading glasses perched at the end of her strong nose, her curly hair swirling around her face like smoke. Lauren had abandoned her campaign to add style to her mother's wardrobe. Marilyn maintained that being an English professor brought certain obligations, one of which was to look slightly eccentric. She claimed it gave her credibility.

"By the way, Mother, I am not being ridiculous about my fat. The lumps on my thighs have graduated from cottage cheese to popcorn. I haven't had the nerve to even look at myself in a swimsuit and summer's almost here!" Lauren leaned into the table and sipped the coffee her mother set before her. "My big mistake is having such a skinny friend. Maybe I should dump Janaan and hang around fat people. At last—a painless way to look thin!"

Marilyn set the plate of French toast in front of Lauren, poured herself a cup of coffee, and settled into a chair across from her daughter. "It is just too early in the morning to listen to this 'I'm so fat' nonsense. You're a beautiful, healthy-looking girl. . . ."

"Healthy! As in a horse? Why don't you just call me obese and get it over with!"

"Lauren, please. You look fine. Trust me when I tell

you Janaan would look better with a few more pounds."

Lauren shook her head. "Janaan is perfect. She's thin and petite, a size five while I'm a size twelve. Case closed."

Marilyn tried to keep the edge from her voice. "I wish you'd believe me when I say you look better than she does."

"You're my mother. God pays you to say things like that," Lauren said, taking a bite of French toast. "Besides, you don't have to get so testy, Mother. I thought I was supposed to be able to tell you how I feel."

"You can!" Marilyn said. "But it goes both ways. So now I'll tell you how I feel. You and Janaan worry far too much about your looks, and not nearly enough about important issues. You and she are more than just bodies. You're young women with minds. Use your brains more and worry about your thighs less!"

"That's easy for you to say. You're not out there being sized up all day," Lauren snapped. "In the real world, people are judged by their looks. Cute guys date cute girls—that's just the way it is."

"Has it ever occurred to you that you've been chasing the wrong type of fellow? Just because a boy is handsome doesn't mean he's a nice person. I know of lots of wonderful young men. . . ."

"Those 'wonderful young men' you're so fond of look like they belong to a different species. I would at least like to date a member of the human race."

Marilyn frowned. "Fine. Make a joke, Laurie. Go

after the athletes who can't grunt more than two syllables."

"Look, Mother, throwing a football does not make someone a mental defective. You're prejudiced against people who look good. It's not a sin to want to be better, thinner, the best you can be."

"I just want you to consider what a person has to offer from the inside," Marilyn cried. "Believe me, the body turns to mush before you know it, and if you choose a mate with mush for brains . . ."

"We're not even talking about mates—this entire conversation started because I want to lose weight."

"The conversation started because you want to look like Janaan."

"I know you want to help, Mother," Lauren said, bristling, "and the world would be a better place if we all thought like you, but I'm not sure you know what's really important."

Her mother put down her coffee mug and glared at Lauren. "Suppose you tell me. I can't imagine how I've lived forty-nine years and raised two other children without knowing."

Exasperation welled inside Lauren. It was useless to talk to her mother about things like appearance, because it always ended in a debate. When faced with the choice, Lauren chose the easy way out: retreat.

"I've got to go," she said, glancing at the kitchen clock for emphasis. "I don't want to be late and I still have to shower."

Marilyn looked at her daughter, perched and ready

to run. She took a deep breath, blew it slowly between her teeth, then relaxed into her chair. Her face softened. "I'm sorry, honey. I guess I came on a little strong. Forgive your old curmudgeon of a mother. I'll save the crusading for my students. Look, you still have some time, so sit down and finish your breakfast, okay?"

Lauren studied her mother, decided the worst was over, then settled back and took another bite. The warm sunlight bent off the jars filled with sweet pea, hyacinth, and crocus starts, creating little rainbows along the windowsill. The clock ticked comfortingly against the hum of the refrigerator. If her mother didn't want to fight, she was in no hurry to leave. She liked to begin her mornings slowly and comfortably.

Marilyn reached across the table to take Lauren's hand. "Listen, sweetie, I know you'd like to drop this subject, but let me leave you with a final thought. Janaan is a beautiful girl, but so are you. It worries me when you compare yourself to her as though she were perfection incarnate. She isn't. In fact, from what I've seen lately, she looks half-starved. Does she eat properly?"

Freeing her hand, Lauren slid off the bench and padded across the floor for a glass of water. "She eats all the time, even though it's healthy food instead of good stuff." She sipped slowly, then said, "She's just disciplined. And speaking of Janaan, you'll never believe who volunteered to come baby-sitting with me today at the Blooms."

Marilyn looked incredulously at Lauren. "I thought

Janaan was never going to baby-sit again after little Adam died."

"That's what she told me. It surprised me, too."

Marilyn rubbed her temple and lowered her head. Lauren could see springy white strands in her mother's hair. "Let's see, how long has it been since that happened, six months?"

"Um-hmmm. Adam died in December."

"Six months. Well, that's not very long. Especially when you consider the way it happened."

Janaan's baby brother Adam was only five months old when he died of sudden infant death syndrome. Janaan had been baby-sitting when she found him, cold and lifeless, his tiny hand still clutching a teddy-bear rattle. Adam was a beautiful baby, with soft, honey-colored ringlets and large, gray-blue eyes. His pale coloring came from his American mother, who was as blond and fair as Lauren. Adam's dimpled smile and chubby thighs had reminded Lauren of the cherubs that float on the ceiling of the Sistine Chapel. It seemed impossible that such a perfect baby could die of crib death.

She'd stood next to Janaan when they buried the tiny coffin, held her hand while the mullah prayed and chanted toward Mecca, hugged her stiff body when the casket was lowered into the frosted earth. Their breath had made little puffs of steam in the winter air. Lauren had felt Janaan flinch when clods of earth were tossed onto the wooden coffin. And yet with all the raw pain she knew throbbed inside her friend, Lauren had never once seen Janaan cry.

No one had expected Janaan to come right back to school, but she had. "It's better if I don't think too much," she'd said. After a while, she'd seemed like her old self, although she refused to baby-sit and never went near a child under two.

"I think it's very healthy for Janaan to baby-sit again. It must mean she's trying to work through her feelings," Marilyn said softly. "Death is hard to face anytime, but when a baby dies—well, it's a very different kind of pain. There's no comfort in it."

"Other than not baby-sitting, she seems to have handled Adam's dying really well. Better than I could have if he were my brother. Jan's always been able to deal with problems."

At least Lauren had thought so, until yesterday when she'd found that picture in their locker.

"Well, that may be," Marilyn told her, "but people don't heal on a schedule, and they don't always do it where we can see."

Lauren sighed. "I know."

She stared past her mother, through the window and into the daylight outside. Her gaze wandered to the freshly turned earth of her mother's vegetable garden. It reminded her of the cemetery. Of things buried. Of Adam. She shuddered. Something inside rebelled at the thought of being dragged into Janaan's depression.

"What time is your sitting job today?" Marilyn asked, breaking into her thoughts.

"In an hour. And I'd better get going! I still have to take a shower, plus pick up Janny!"

Her mother pushed back from the table. "Before you go, I want you to know I'm sorry about lecturing you. You're a good person, Laurie."

"Not as good as I should be. Thanks for the breakfast, Mom," she called over her shoulder.

"No problem. Just remember you're the one cooking tonight!"

3

Janaan was waiting outside, arms crossed over her chest, when Lauren pulled up. Her just-washed hair had been pulled into a puff at the top, and her mouth was carefully carved in bright scarlet. Little pastel hearts dotted her crisp cotton shirt, which hung loosely over stone-washed jeans. As she raised her hand to wave, three heart bracelets slipped down her arm. She looked terrific, as usual. Lauren wished she'd worn some earrings.

"Good morning!" Lauren called cheerily through her passenger window.

"Hi."

Janaan sounded sullen as she slid into the car. She didn't look at Lauren.

"You're sure you want to spend your day off at the Blooms?" Lauren asked, backing out. "You seem less than enthusiastic."

"You wouldn't believe what happened in there. You just wouldn't believe it! My dad forbade me to come with you."

Lauren slammed on her brakes.

"Keep driving. I told him I didn't care what he wanted—I was going. Go on!" Janaan ordered.

Lauren moved forward slowly, anticipating a retreat at any time.

"Aren't you going to ask me why?" Before Lauren could say a word, Janaan raged ahead. "He said he would not have his daughter sitting for any Jewish child. Can you believe that? I told him he could just try and stop me! I said, 'I can do whatever I want and there's not a damn thing you can do about it!'"

"You swore at your father?" Lauren asked, astounded. "I can't believe you swore and lived to tell about it. Maybe you shouldn't come." If there was one person Lauren didn't want to offend, it was Abdul Kashad. He was small and husky, with fierce black eyes and a raw, intense face. Not many people scared her, but he did.

"No way, I'm going. Drive!"

Lauren kept glancing at her rearview mirror, half expecting Abdul Kashad to come speeding after them. She saw a woman yanking weeds from her garden, and several men pushing mowers, but the street itself remained empty. Lauren relaxed as she pulled onto the main road.

"I'm really sorry you started your morning like that," she began, hoping to shift Janaan's mood. "But let's not let your dad ruin our fun. We've got a whole day ahead of us. Did I tell you what happened in the lunchroom yesterday? Some guy came up and grabbed me from behind because he thought I was Cynthia Walker!"

"How could he mistake you for Cynthia when you weren't lying down?" Janaan asked wryly.

Lauren laughed. "Now that's the catty friend I know and love. But let's not be too mean. I heard Cynthia's not going to college, and she's having trouble landing a job because they say she doesn't have enough experience."

"I'm sure the football team would give her references."

"Janaan!"

"Sorry. I'm in a bad mood. Mind if I turn on the radio?"

"Sure," Lauren answered. "You know, this must be the morning for scenes, Janny. I just had a—how shall I say it?—discussion with my mother. She thinks I go after the wrong type. She thinks I should be happy with the geeks she picks for me—and I almost spilled the goods on that slime Barry she set me up with."

"You mean the one who attacked you at the drive-in? You didn't tell me it was your mother that put you two together."

"Yep. She did. He was some professor's son, and, oh, the stories I could tell her! I don't know why she thinks ugly means no hormones."

Janaan asked, "Why didn't you tell her what happened? Maybe then she'd back off."

"Because you don't know my mother. If I told her what really happened, she'd have my dad and the professor and the slime called together for a big confrontation. She still sees me as the helpless baby of the family." Lauren shrugged. "Giving my mother information can be dangerous."

"Well," Janaan said, "at least she's out recruiting for you. Dating is absolute poison in my family. My dad thinks two teenagers of the opposite sex can't be in the same room without tearing each other's clothes off."

"Why is that? Is it some Middle Eastern attitude, or is it because—"

"It's because he's a tyrant. No offense, Laurie, but I'm not in the mood to analyze why my father is so obnoxious. It's just the way he is, okay? Are we here already?"

"How'd you know that?"

"Because of my incredible powers of observation. You're slowing down, and the mailbox says Bloom."

Lauren parked in front of a house that was perfectly neat and manicured, nestled among a string of impeccable middle-class homes. Along the walkway, red and yellow tulips marched in military rows, edged precisely by well-clipped Bermuda grass. Sculptured trees stood in symmetrical groups like living statues. In his spare time David Bloom coaxed buds and annihilated bugs with relish.

The door opened and Miriam Bloom motioned them inside. "Please come in, girls," she said quickly. Her voice sounded harried. "I had a call so I didn't get a chance to feed Rachael. I just changed her, though, so you won't have to for a little while. Oh, we might be gone an extra hour—would that cause you any kind of problem, Lauren?"

Lauren shook her head no. She had to listen carefully whenever Miriam talked, because she spoke very fast and usually while doing two or more things. Miriam looked as if she were barely out of college, although Lauren knew she and David had been married almost fifteen years before they had Rachael.

"Fine with me. Is another hour okay with you?" Lauren asked, turning to Janaan.

"Sure."

"Oh, I'm sorry, I haven't even introduced you two properly. I asked if I could bring a friend, but I didn't tell you who. Miriam Bloom, this is Janaan Kashad— Janaan, Miriam."

The smile on Miriam's face froze.

"Kashad. That name is most familiar. Are you by any chance related to Abdul Kashad?"

"He's my father," Janaan answered. "Do you know him?"

"I know of him. He's very political, isn't he." It was more a statement than a question. Miriam fingered the gold Star of David that dangled from her neck. "Does your father know you're here in my house?"

"I told him I was coming," Janaan answered, defiant. "If you'd like me to leave . . ."

"Is Mr. Bloom here?" Lauren broke in. She sensed the tension between Miriam and Janaan, as though they were conversing wordlessly about something Lauren didn't understand.

"I—what did you say?" Miriam asked, finally looking at Lauren.

"Mr. Bloom. I was just wondering where he is."

"He's already left for the office. And remember, Lauren, call us Miriam and David. You're making me feel very old."

"If you don't want me to stay," Janaan began, "maybe you could drop me off on your way. Otherwise I don't have a ride home."

"No. No, it's fine." Miriam's words were clipped. "If you would like to be here, I would like to have you stay."

A light touch on her foot made Lauren look down. "Since when did you learn to crawl?" she asked, bending to pick up six-month-old Rachael.

"She started pulling herself around about two days ago. She could use a bath if you have time to get to it. Don't worry if you can't." Whatever the problem was, it had been resolved somehow. Miriam looked from Janaan to Lauren.

"Well," she said, "the number's by the phone if you need me. I'd better run or I'll be late. Call if there's any trouble."

"We'll be fine," Lauren answered.

"Good-bye then. Shalom."

In a whirlwind of perfume and papers Miriam breezed out the door, stopping only to give Rachael a light kiss before she was gone. The house felt suddenly dead, as though its life had been swept out of it.

Lauren turned to stare at Janaan. "What on earth was that all about?"

"She obviously knows who my father is." Janaan collapsed into an overstuffed chair.

"What about your father? I felt like I was watching a foreign movie without subtitles."

"It's politics, Laurie. Welcome to the wonderful world of politics. As usual, my own father is in the middle of this, and like I said, I don't want to talk about him."

"Sure. Whatever." Lauren knew better than to pursue the subject, because when Janaan clammed up, nothing could pry her open.

There was a tug, then a sharp pull on Lauren's hair. "Ouch! No, Rachael, let go," she cried as she unwound strands of her own hair from Rachael's tiny fist. "Go see smart Janny who put her hair on top of her head, away from your death grip."

Lauren looked cautiously at Janaan, searching for a sense of how she felt with a small child so near. Their eyes met.

"If you're wondering how I'm doing with Rachael, I'm okay. Although I wish you had warned me how much she looks like Adam." Janaan sighed. "I never thought I could feel this way, but the old saying is true. Life goes on. I can't keep avoiding babies the rest of my life. People insist on having them."

Walking slowly toward her friend, Lauren asked, "Would you like to hold her?"

"You don't waste any time, do you? Sure, I'll take her." Janaan held out her arms. Rachael rolled into them, stared solemnly at Janaan's face for a moment, then caught hold of one of the heart-shaped bracelets.

"Here, sweetie, let me get that for you," Janaan said softly. She slipped the heart off her wrist and gave it to Rachael. "That was one of Adam's favorite toys, too."

Holding her gently, as though Rachael were made of spun glass, Janaan lowered herself into the chair and rested a cheek on Rachael's soft, wheat-colored hair. Lauren felt her throat tighten. The two made a ghostly image, an uncanny recreation of Janaan cradling baby Adam.

So many times in the past, as Janaan's hair had brushed against Adam's honey-gold curls, dark against light, Lauren had wondered how they could be brother and sister. Now, for a heartbeat, it seemed time had stopped and Adam was back again.

"What's wrong, Laurie? You look spooked."

"I don't know, it's just . . ."

"She reminds you of my little brother. It's strange, but instead of hurting it feels kind of nice to remember him. She's about the same age as he was when . . . when he died." She looked away. "I wish things had been different. But I guess I was lucky to have him even for a little while. Here, you take her."

Janaan's eyes misted as she passed Rachael back.

"Janny, is Adam the reason you've been so down? I mean, I was thinking about the picture and then I thought of Adam."

Shaking her head, Janaan said, "No, that's not it. I'm not over it completely, but I've accepted his death. And remember, you promised not to read too much into what I did. It's not because of Adam, but to tell you the truth, I feel a little drained and don't want to go into anything right now. Okay?"

"Sure," Lauren answered, bouncing Rachael on her knee. "Hey, how about if we take a walk? This little monkey is a fussy eater, which is the real reason Miriam didn't feed her before she left. Fresh air usually makes her hungry."

Janaan looked away. "No, you go on. I think I'll sit here for a while."

"Come on," Lauren urged. "We can see if there are any cute neighbors around here. A baby is the perfect opener!"

"I'm not in the mood. You go on and I promise I'll be better company by the time you get back. I just want to sit here and think."

Rachael strained in Lauren's arms, reaching toward the stroller that stood next to the door.

"Okay you little toad, you win." Lauren laughed. "You hear the word *walk* and it's all over. We'll just go around the block, Janny. Sure you don't want to come?"

"Positive."

"Okay, then. If I meet any fabulous guy you get his friend, and friends of cute guys are usually reptilian." Carefully, she strapped Rachael into the stroller. "That's my final threat, Janny!"

"I'll take my chances. Besides, I haven't read this *People* magazine. I'll see you in a bit."

As Lauren pushed the stroller down the walk, she thought about leaving her friend behind. What was Janaan going to tell her when she got back? Unease filled her as she pictured the deep, scarlike gouge running through the photograph. If the problem wasn't Adam, then maybe Janaan would confront her about something she'd done. Mentally she reviewed scenes of the two of them, searching for a clue, for any hint of what she might have done to upset Janaan.

Since Adam died, the two of them spent more and more time at the Taylor home. Maybe that was it. Maybe Janaan felt as though Lauren didn't like her parents, or her house, or her brothers. She bit her lip and tried to remember. No, it was Janaan who'd insisted they do everything at Lauren's house.

It had to be something else. But what? She felt a sudden surge of irritation. The whole thing was ridiculous. Why was she trying to blame herself for Janaan's foul temper? And why did she always have to wait until Janaan was in the mood to talk?

Lauren began to walk faster. Somehow, subtly, the balance in their friendship had shifted. Well, no more. She deserved an explanation, whether Janaan was ready to open up or not. Rounding the corner, she stared ahead resolutely. It was time to talk.

4

Lauren looked at the front door of the Bloom home. Her resolve to confront Janaan had weakened with every step, and the long walk had made her damp with perspiration. Even Rachael seemed sticky, with little cracks of baby powder congealed in her joints. Lauren glanced at her watch, then looked at the baby.

"Do you want to stay outside a little longer, Rach? How about you and me lying out for a while on the grass?"

Rachael sucked on her fist and smiled.

"I'll take that as a yes. I bet it's going to reach ninety degrees today, so we might as well enjoy the sunshine before it gets too beastly hot. And, of course, I'm stalling. But you don't know that, do you?"

She placed Rachael stomach-down on a blanket and dived beside her. A breeze rustled the leaves and branches, creating a rushing, rhythmic sound, almost like waves on a beach. Someone somewhere was playing heavy metal; the beat blended with the growl from a distant lawn mower.

As she lay stretched on the lawn, a dark blue sedan drove slowly past. It stopped, seeming to hover in the center of the street before continuing on its way. Lauren felt her breath catch—the car looked exactly like Abdul Kashad's. Could he have followed Janaan here? Was he so angry at her that he'd resort to spy games?

Lauren jumped to her feet and ran to the edge of the curb, straining to get a look at the driver, but the smoked glass made it impossible to see inside. As she squinted to make out the license plate number, the sedan disappeared around a corner.

"Darn! I only got the first three letters. SEF. I wonder if that was Mr. Kashad?" she asked Rachael. "You know, Rach"—Lauren dropped next to the baby—"my friend has a very strange father. I'm glad you've got your daddy, and I'm especially glad I've got mine."

As she stroked Rachael's hair, Lauren thought of her own father, a tall, wiry man with hair so thin she could see the shine of his scalp. Quiet and gentle-mannered, he'd always made her feel safe, insulated, as though her home and her family were a cocoon wrapped tightly around her. At times she felt suffocated and couldn't wait to break free from his protection, and yet, when she saw the way Abdul Kashad treated Janaan, Lauren knew she was lucky.

"If my dad didn't yell at me, I'd swear I was invisible," Janaan had told her once. "It must be because I was born female. Women are not an Arab's favorite life-form, you know. They'd rather have a son or a camel."

Lauren hadn't answered. Often enough she'd seen evidence of her friend's complaint, especially since Adam's death. Once she'd followed Janaan into her father's study.

"May I borrow a credit card, Father?" Janaan had asked. "There's an unbelievable sale at Krystie's." Her voice had faltered as she'd added, "Mom said it was okay."

Abdul Kashad's eyes had smoldered disapproval as he'd opened his wallet, removed his Visa card, and given it to Janaan. The billfold had clapped shut in his hand.

Then Lauren witnessed a sudden metamorphosis. The fire left Abdul Kashad's eyes and his face softened. "Ishmael, Jacob, come in."

Janaan's younger brothers stood grinning from the doorway. "What is it you want?" their father had asked, motioning them in. "Money? I'm sorry; your sister has bled me dry. Come, come closer." He'd reached out a hand to ruffle Ishmael's dark hair. "What else can I give to you and your brother?"

That's when she'd caught sight of Janaan, shoulders hunched, watching her father with a hungry look in her eyes.

It isn't fair, Lauren thought, the way he treats Janaan. How would it be to have a father like Abdul Kashad? To be forbidden, controlled, ignored. She tried to imagine herself in Janaan's place, but the picture wouldn't come. Her own dad was too mild.

A voice broke into her thoughts. "I see you have your baby out, too."

Lauren sat up and shielded her eyes from the sun. A woman in her late forties pushed a carriage up the walkway and stopped in front of her.

"I can't stand to be inside on a morning like this," the woman said. "The birds were calling me through my window—come out come out come out."

The woman was beautiful, with autumn-red hair woven in three subtle shades of color, and soft brown eyes as wide as a doe's. Although roughly the age of Lauren's mother, her complexion had none of the character. The lines on her face were as thin and fine as a spider's web.

"My name is Marjorie. My baby loves the sunshine, but I'm afraid she'll burn in this heat. What's your baby's name?"

"This is Rachael Bloom, and I'm Lauren Taylor."

"Oh, you've got different last names. Is your baby adopted? Well, that makes her extra special, too."

"She's not mine, but I wouldn't mind if she were, she's such a sweetie," Lauren said, as Rachael inched off the blanket. When Lauren grabbed her to pull her back, Rachael let out a piercing scream.

"Don't stop her from coming to me. I love babies," the woman said brightly. She hurried over and scooped Rachael into her arms.

"Aren't you a sweet one? Aren't you beautiful! You're a special little angel." Rachael's head bobbed and weaved as the woman bounced her on her hip. "My little girl's a redhead. That's why I dyed my hair. See? So we could match." She fingered wisps of Rachael's golden hair. "I like your color much better. I think I like you even better than my baby." She kissed Rachael and squeezed her, then smiled brilliantly at Lauren. "Can I take her home with me? How much do you want for her?"

Pricks of apprehension crept over Lauren's skin. This lady must have a bizarre sense of humor. In all her experience with mothers, Lauren had never found one that fussed over a stranger's baby while her own child lay ignored in a carriage.

"Money has never been a problem. I've got money," the woman added.

"Her mom wouldn't sell her," Lauren said, deciding to play along. She rose to her feet cautiously, still trying to believe everything was all right. As she stood she could see Marjorie tense.

"But I want her!" Marjorie began to sway back and forth, her white cotton skirt ruffling in the breeze. Long, polished nails dug into Rachael's back, making her whimper.

"Well, I think it's about time for us to go in now," Lauren said slowly, trying to keep her voice casual. "Come on, Rachael."

With a wrenching movement, Marjorie twisted away.

Lauren glanced quickly toward the house, but Janaan was nowhere in sight. She could feel her heart hammer. "Let me have the baby now."

The woman shook her head, clutching Rachael tighter.

"*Please* let me have Rachael!" Lauren demanded. Marjorie's smile had faded. Her brows knit together and her rose-colored lips thinned to a straight line.

"Now look, I have to take Rachael in. Give her to me!" Lauren made a lunge toward Rachael, but the woman shot out one hand and screamed, "*No!*" with such force that it stopped Lauren dead. The cry startled Rachael, whose whimpers turned to howls. When she reached for Lauren, Marjorie pulled her violently back.

"Don't cry, little one. Marjorie's here to take care of you now," she said between hard kisses that left lipstick moons across the baby's cheeks. Lauren's arms hung taut at her sides. What should she do? Where was Janaan? She scanned the street frantically, but it seemed strangely deserted.

A flicker of movement caught her eye. Across the street, a man watched from a white truck crammed with gardening tools. His thin face filled with crooked teeth as he smiled at her, a question in his eyes. Lauren's heart leaped. Did he know? Did he understand that a crazy woman had stolen Rachael and refused to give her back? She raised her hand in a plea for help, praying he would comprehend, but he sat unmoving.

Fear and anger built inside her. In a neighborhood full of people, she felt utterly alone. Alone and terrified.

"Listen, I want Rachael or I'll call the police. Do you hear? Give her to me *now!*"

There was no response. The woman's eyes, her entire being, seemed focused solely on Rachael.

"You're such a pretty little thing. I wish my baby was as pretty as you."

Marjorie finally looked at Lauren, her eyes clouding. "But you don't always have a choice. Babies are so hard to get nowadays. Would you like to see my first baby, my Irene?"

The woman reached into the carriage to pull back a quilt embroidered with grinning bears. "I have to shield her from the sun," she murmured. "Her skin's so fair."

Lauren looked in and gasped. Two stiff cloth arms reached up at her. Two blank, painted eyes stared from a plastic face, framed in orange yarn hair. Irene was nothing but a Cabbage Patch doll!

Rachael writhed against Marjorie's stomach, but Marjorie only held her tighter, oblivious to the movement and to her cries.

"Help is needed here?"

Relief rushed through Lauren. She'd gotten through to the man in the truck! He was coming to help her.

"Help is needed?" he called again as he hurried toward them. Thin and hollow-chested, he had stringy black hair and an accent Lauren couldn't place. Sweat had left dark circles on his green workman's uniform, and the heavy canvas gloves he wore were dirt-encrusted and streaked with stains. He glanced up and down the empty street before he approached Marjorie.

"The baby is needed by you?" he asked softly, pointing from Marjorie to Lauren. Marjorie watched him intently, unmoving, like a steely-eyed cat with a twitchy tail, while Rachael's screams grew louder. The man took a small step toward the baby and stretched out his hand.

Suddenly Marjorie snapped to attention. "Stay away—she's mine! I didn't ask you to come. Go away!"

The man took another small step. "This one is very pretty."

"Go away!"

"A baby is like an animal. They know when to love." He leaned closer to Marjorie. "Look for yourself—this one love you."

Lauren could see Marjorie soften. The strong line of her jaw melted, and for the first time her eyes focused on the workman as he sidled nearer.

"You can see that she loves me? You can see it?" Marjorie's voice sounded weak.

He was only inches from her now, and he slowly reached out his hand until it rested lightly on Rachael's hair. His eyes locked with Marjorie's, the man's coal-black, hers wild. She seemed mesmerized by him. Sweat shone on his umber skin, but he stayed calm. Lauren's heart felt raw in her chest. She watched breathlessly as the man eased himself in front of Rachael, knowing he was ready to make his move.

"Marjorie!"

A well-dressed man as immaculate as Marjorie walked briskly up to the three of them. "Marjorie, I see you've found a friend. But it's time to come home now."

He pried her fingers, bent like claws, from around Rachael's stomach and back. Marjorie stood agitated and confused as he lifted Rachael from her arms.

"I'm sorry if she frightened you. Sometimes she gets too motherly when she sees a small baby like that one," he told Lauren, handing a wailing Rachael to her before he turned back to Marjorie. "Let's go now."

The workman in the green uniform glanced from Lauren to Marjorie, shrugged his shoulders, then backed away to saunter toward his truck, as though all the ugliness had been resolved once Rachael was returned. But Lauren's relief was overcome by indignation.

"Just a minute. Is that all you can say—she gets too motherly? That woman took Rachael and wouldn't give her back, not even with Rachael screaming and trying to get to me. And all you say is 'Let's go now.' What is she doing walking around loose?"

The man turned to her, his expression cold. "I hardly think I need to explain anything to some overwrought teenager. If you want answers, ask the Blooms. They know all about Marjorie."

"Is it time to go home now, Jim?" Marjorie asked, placing both hands on the carriage handle.

"Yes, let's take Irene and go." His silver-tipped head bent as he kissed Marjorie. She returned his kiss, then gently placed the quilt over the whole doll so that not one strand of yarn hair could be seen.

Marjorie smiled tenderly at the small mound in the

bottom of the carriage before she turned to Lauren. "Good-bye. And take good care of that baby of yours. You have to be so very careful with babies."

The carriage made a clack-clack sound as it rolled over the grooves in the sidewalk.

5

Lauren raced through the front door and slammed it hard behind her. Holding Rachael tightly against her, she maneuvered the dead bolt into place, then leaned against the door and collapsed. Her sharp breathing was the only sound to break the stillness. *People* magazine lay unopened on the couch. The television flashed silently, but Janaan was nowhere to be seen. Lauren took a deep breath.

"Janaan!" she yelled. Her voice sounded harsh in her own ears. "Janaan! Come here!"

Rachael wriggled against her grip, tired of being confined so tightly for so long. Lauren grabbed one of Rachael's blankets and tossed it to the floor, then carefully placed her on it.

"Are you okay, Rachael? You lie right there where I can see you."

Janaan rounded the hall corner and froze. "Laurie? What's wrong? You look like you're sick. Is Rachael all right?" Her eyes darted until she found Rachael quietly chewing a corner of her blanket.

"Where were you? This crazy woman grabbed Rachael. . . ."

"A crazy woman? Come here and sit down. What are you talking about?"

Two cups of herbal tea later, Lauren was still wound up. Janaan had listened quietly as she went over and over her story—what she'd done, what she hadn't done, what Marjorie had said—until Lauren's throat felt dry and tight from talking so much.

"What do you think, Janny?" she asked again. "Should I call the police or the mental health people or something? They shouldn't let sick women like her wander loose looking for babies to steal."

Janaan sat on the floor beside Rachael, legs crossed, head bent forward. She seemed engrossed in pulling a spot of dried cereal off one of Rachael's stuffed animals.

"Hand me the phone, Janny. I think I'd better call the police."

"Why don't you just let it go, Lauren?" Janaan was still intent on the toy. "She really didn't hurt you, and Rachael's fine, and, well, I think if you called the police she'd probably get into a lot of trouble and . . ."

"Are you kidding?" Lauren flared. "I wouldn't care if they locked her in a rubber room for the rest of her life. She kidnapped Rachael! Haven't you heard a word I've said?"

"Look, Lauren, the lady sounds like she has a lot of problems, but she doesn't seem to be an ax murderer or anything." Janaan spoke softly. "Don't you feel even a little sorry for someone who drags a stupid Cabbage

Patch doll around and pretends it's real? Plus the fact that you don't know what she was about to do next. She might have given Rachael back on her own if her husband hadn't come."

"She also might have taken Rachael away and strangled her before anyone could stop her!" Lauren shot back. "You know, Janaan, you sound nice and open-minded here in this living room, but you weren't standing there trying to deal with a crazy person all by yourself. That workman knew I needed help—he could tell she was nuts. I got more support from a total stranger than I get from my supposed best friend."

Lauren saw resentment ignite and then burn out in Janaan's face before she reached to pat Lauren's knee. "Don't get mad, Laurie. It does sound scary and I don't know what I would have done if it had been me. I just can't get over how sad the whole thing is." She sighed and turned back to Rachael's stuffed animal. "Anyway, if you think calling the police is the best thing, go ahead. I'll get you the phone." Her knees cracked as she unwound her small frame and stood.

Lauren stared at the particles of dust dancing in light-streaks that knifed through the curtains. She loved this room, all brown and beige, with splashes of green where Miriam's jungle of plants hung. In Lauren's home, every surface was smooth and shiny. The wood was polished cherry, with lots of gleaming brass and glass. Here, clay pots and wood carvings crowded oak tabletops, and every surface seemed nappy. She usually felt peaceful here, but now her emotions were as tangled as the Jerusalem cherry vines that twisted for life in the sunshine.

"Lauren, the police are on the line. Are you ready?"

Suddenly the tension inside her burst into a wash of tears. Janaan was right—Marjorie was pathetic. She needed to let it go. "Hang up, Janny," Lauren sobbed.

"Are you sure?"

"Just hang up. I don't want to talk to anybody anymore." She buried her face into the couch and cried hard. Hot tears disappeared into the rough fabric, mingling with the smell of David Bloom's pipe tobacco. When she felt Janaan's strong arms circle her in a tight hug, Lauren turned and clung to her.

"You're doing the right thing," Janaan whispered. "Now forget it. Okay?"

"Okay." Lauren gulped a few times, then pulled free. "I'm glad you were here. I've never had to deal with such a weird person before. I was really scared."

"I know. But if you ever see her again, tell her her baby is just a little doll!"

Lauren groaned, then wiped her eyes with the palms of her hands.

"Or," Janaan declared, shaking her finger, "you should say, 'Marjorie, that baby of yours eats way too much. Why, that child looks stuffed!' "

As she grabbed a nearby tissue, Lauren sniffed. "Janaan, those are the worst jokes I've ever heard you make since I've known you."

"Maybe. But you're smiling! And that's better than leaving mascara trails all over the Blooms' couch."

"Oh, no! Where?"

"Right there. Don't panic, they'll wash out. I think it was good for you to cry—it cleanses the soul."

"If crying's so great, why don't you ever do it? Nothing seems to rattle you the way it does me. You must think I'm a baby."

Janaan smiled. "The only baby I see is the one falling asleep in the corner."

"But I haven't even fed her!" Lauren protested, jumping to her feet.

"I'm sure she'll be fine. Why don't you let me put her down while you wash your face."

After crossing to where Rachael lay sleeping, Janaan bent down and gently gathered the baby into her arms. Lauren disappeared into the bathroom, dampened some toilet tissue, and wiped black smudges from beneath her eyes.

"Well, I'll say one thing, Janny," she called loudly, "you really are a great baby-sitter. Not only for Rachael, but for me, too. I was so happy when I finally saw your face. Where were you when I first came in? I about died when I couldn't find you."

Janaan poked her head out the nursery doorway and held a finger to pursed lips. "Shhh. She's asleep."

"Already? She usually wakes up whenever I move her."

"Well, she didn't for me."

"Did you wipe off her face?" Lauren asked, tiptoeing down the hallway. "She had red smears all over her cheeks."

Shaking her head, Janaan moved aside as Lauren entered the nursery. The blinds had been shut, and in the dimness the room's pale pinks and yellows muted to a soft gray.

Gently, with the end of a damp tissue, Lauren rubbed the last traces of Marjorie's lipstick from the baby's cheek. She wound a little lamb musical toy and set it beside the baby in her crib. The lullaby tinkled comfortingly in the stillness, but Rachael was already asleep.

"She's out. I can't believe how tired she is today," Lauren whispered as she motioned Janaan out the door.

They made their way to the den and sprawled in front of the television set.

"They've got cable," Lauren mentioned. "Miriam said we could help ourselves to the food. Maybe there's a good movie on."

"Tough job," Janaan muttered.

The two of them settled in with a box of powdered doughnuts and watched the end of a Clint Eastwood movie. After the last credit, Janaan rolled to her knees and stood up.

"Why don't you gather all those crumbs while I go check on Rachael?" she suggested.

"Sure," Lauren answered, "only be careful not to wake her. That makes her really crabby."

Lauren squatted to pinch the crumbs from the carpet. "Doughnut dust is more like it. I think we're going to have to vacuum," she called down the hall to Janaan. "Is she up? Jan?" Hearing no answer, she straightened and headed for the nursery. "Janny, are you in there? Is Rachael awake?"

"Lauren, call the paramedics!" Janaan screamed. "Rachael isn't breathing. Oh my God, I think she's dead!"

6

Dusk came creeping into Lauren's room, casting quiet shadows that lengthened unnoticed in the stillness. Head pressed against her window, she watched the flowers gray, then dissolve into evening. The funeral had been two days before. Lauren felt as though the color was disappearing from her soul the way the blossoms were fading into the dark of night.

No toy had smothered Rachael, no blanket had strangled her. The pediatrician called it crib death and allowed the Blooms to bury their baby, in accordance with their custom, by sundown. She was gone. Swallowed into the earth, to be reduced by time to a handful of dust.

Lauren hadn't gone to Rachael's burial. She could never, ever face Miriam or David Bloom again, couldn't bear to see the pain in their eyes as they tossed earth onto the coffin of their only child. Her father had come home early that night to try and explain Rachael's death, telling Lauren people are born to die and only God knew the right time to call Rachael home.

She had glared at him and said, "God wouldn't kill Rachael." He'd rubbed his forehead, pressing the furrows deeper between his eyes until his skin burned red.

When he finally spoke, he sounded weary. "What I told you doesn't help, does it? Honey, we don't always understand, but God doesn't make mistakes." When he pulled her close, she smelled sweet traces of aftershave mingling with the bite of sweat.

He had tried to soothe her, but an epitaph she'd seen the day Adam died haunted her, quelling any comfort she might have found in her father's words.

After Adam's funeral a crowd of relatives had surrounded Janaan, so Lauren had wandered the sections of the cemetery reserved for different religions. A faded insert in a tombstone caught her eye. The oval picture, a black-and-white photo wreathed by fresh snow, showed a baby dressed in a christening gown. She'd crouched down to brush away the flakes and read, IF I HAVE BEEN SO QUICKLY DONE FOR, I WONDER WHAT I WAS BEGUN FOR.

There were no answers, not from God or anyone else. The cold fact was that Rachael had died in her care, and Lauren was left to go over that day and wonder.

The doorbell rang. Voices murmured below, but Lauren didn't care enough to move. Footsteps pounded up the stairs; a moment later Janaan hugged her tightly.

"It's not your fault, Laurie. It's not your fault," she whispered into her hair. "Please don't do this to yourself."

Lauren pulled away and stared at her friend. Janaan

looked cool in a fragile pastel print, a white satin ribbon bowed in her hair, small freshwater pearls dotting her ears. Lauren had to hand it to her: No matter what the crisis, Janaan looked perfect. Lauren was dressed exactly the way she felt, in her grungy gray hole-in-the-knee sweats with the grease stain on the thigh.

"If anyone should understand, it's you," Lauren said tightly. "Rachael is dead. I was in charge."

"And what could you have done, sat by her crib and watched her breathe? Lauren, listen to me. I lost my own brother while I was baby-sitting. I know more than anyone how you feel. There was nothing you could have done. Nothing."

"What about crazy Marjorie? Maybe she did something to Rachael."

"Blaming people doesn't help, Lauren. Marjorie was just a poor sick woman who happened to hold Rachael the day she died. Do you mind if I turn on a light in here? I can barely see you."

The brightness of the light made Lauren wince.

"You look awful. How long have you been up here?"

"I don't know. A while."

"Well," Janaan said, taking her hand, "it's time to get out. I'm taking you to Fred's for pizza, with the blessing of your parents."

"I don't want to . . ."

"Save your breath. I know you don't but it's for your own good. You've got to eat, and we're going to get a large pepperoni with double cheese and garlic bread. Oh, and I brought you your homework. Even though school's almost out, there's a test next week. And one other thing . . ."

Anger broke through the ball of pain Lauren carried inside. Why did everyone expect her to act as if nothing had happened? Her parents had tried to drag her to a movie, and now Janaan babbled about homework. "Rachael is dead," she said, her voice quivering. "Don't you remember? I cry when someone dies. I'm not a little soldier like you are."

She could tell Janaan was stung, but right then she didn't care. It felt good to spill some of the hurt and anger she'd been drowning in the last couple of days. Without a word Janaan began to gather the papers she'd tossed onto Lauren's bed. Her motions jerked with indignation.

"Wait. I'm sorry. I shouldn't have said that. Please don't leave. Janny, I feel so awful. Please stay with me." Lauren covered her face with her hands as fresh tears squeezed between her fingers. "I just can't stand the fact that she died with me taking care of her. I can't help feeling somehow"—her voice choked—"responsible."

Janaan produced a tissue for Lauren, then patted her shoulder. "It's okay. Don't worry. You should have heard the things I yelled at my mother—I guess what goes around comes around. But Laurie, never, ever say I don't care. Just because I'm not crying like you doesn't mean I'm not hurting. I've got my own way of handling things. And even if the voice of God told you differently, I know you'd think there was something you could have done. Which is the other thing I was going to tell you. I've invited some people over to talk to you."

Lauren groaned. "I don't feel like talking to anyone but you. My eyes are so swollen I have bags under bags. Can't you cancel it?"

"No," Janaan said, glancing at her watch. "They'll be here any minute. Now before you get all upset, they're volunteers from the SIDS Foundation—SIDS stands for Sudden Infant Death Syndrome. They'll talk to you about crib death and I want you to listen to what they have to say. They really helped me."

"Do my folks know about this?" Lauren asked, hoping for a way out.

"Yes, they do. Now wipe your nose and come downstairs. After we talk with them we'll skip out for a while and eat, and I guarantee you'll feel better. Okay?"

Lauren sighed in resignation. "Okay, Janny, you win. Let me wash my face and put on a little makeup first."

The doorbell chimed just as Lauren entered her bathroom.

"Too late, they're here. I'll run down and meet them, and you hurry. See you in a minute!"

7

Fred's pizza parlor was crowded, as always on a Friday night, mostly with kids their age. It seemed to take forever to snake through the posts and chains that led to the counter. A knot of girls behind them argued over thick or thin crust, while a couple ahead clung and kissed, blind to everyone but each other. A haze of smoke blended into the smell of peppers and onions, making the atmosphere murky in the dim light. Lauren felt vaguely guilty about being there, surrounded by people who were absorbed with their own lives, oblivious to the fact that little Rachael Bloom was dead.

"Can you believe that?" Janaan moaned, rolling her eyes.

"What?" Suddenly Lauren realized Janaan had been talking to her.

"Cynthia. In gym today."

"Cynthia?"

"Perfect. I just love talking to myself. How much of my soliloquy did you miss?"

"Um, all of it. Sorry. Tell me again and I promise I'll listen."

The line inched forward. Janaan had been chattering since they'd left the Taylors' living room, but Lauren's mind kept drifting to the small, soft-spoken SIDS volunteer and her husband who clutched hands as they shared the pain of their own child's death. A second, younger couple had watched quietly, rarely speaking but nodding in solemn agreement whenever the first couple wavered. Twice Lauren had caught the young woman searching Janaan's face, a question clouding her eyes, but Janny seemed not to notice. Lauren reminded herself to ask if they'd met before.

"I was telling you about the scene in gym today. Cynthia was bouncing away on the trampoline, and I emphasize the word *bounce,* when Ms. Greenley yelled time. Cynthia was getting off when she sort of fell into Greenley. So Greenley got really mad, and Cynthia said, 'I'm sorry, it was just an accident.' Greenley yelled, 'There's a difference between an accident and premeditated stupidity.'" Janaan grinned. "Cynthia put her hands on her hips, looked Greenley right in the eye, and said, 'Which one did your mother say *you* were?'"

Lauren started to giggle.

"I about fell over laughing," Janaan said. "I hope Cynthia graduates before one of the teachers kills her. It's time to order—pepperoni okay with you?"

"Oh. Yeah. Plus garlic bread and a Diet Coke for me."

In spite of herself, Lauren felt her mood lighten. She'd been wrapped in grief and self-doubt, but Janaan was shoving her back into the mainstream. She wished she had Janaan's strength.

They squeezed into the only place left, a small corner table with crumpled napkins and crumbs scattered across the top. Lauren yanked off a slice of pizza and gave it a voracious bite.

"You're eating, and I'll take that as a good sign," Janaan said. "I knew taking you out would work."

"I do feel better. Thanks."

"Before we drop the subject for the rest of the night, I wanted to ask you about the SIDS people. What did you think?"

The volunteers. Lauren could almost hear them, the low, rumbly voices of the men and the soothing tones of the women. Everyone in that room had suffered the same incredible loss. They had taunted themselves with guilt, just as Lauren had, until they came to grips with the randomness of crib death. Their bond of understanding touched her, healing the raw edge of pain she'd carried inside.

"You were right, Jan," Lauren said softly. "I needed to see them. I guess everyone thinks they're to blame when something like this happens." She paused. "Oh, I remember what I was going to ask—have you ever met that one lady before? The one that kept staring at you?"

Janaan's eyes widened. "Who was staring at me?"

"The woman on my left, the one with the short blond hair. Every once in a while I'd catch her looking you over like she knew you, but she never said anything. Did she talk to you when Adam died?"

Janaan frowned in concentration. "No, Lois and Jack were there, but the support couple was black. That blond's face seemed familiar, but I just can't place where we met. Do you remember her name?"

Lauren shook her head. "I wasn't paying attention when we were introduced. It was Carol or Cathy or something like that."

"Cathy sounds right, but I wasn't paying attention, either. Oh, well, it'll come to me. Now, the subject is closed. What else would you like to talk about?"

Lauren unwrapped her straw and jabbed it into her Coke. The couple who had been kissing in the pizza line hunched together at the next table, feeding each other pizza as though it were wedding cake. The girl's dark hair hung in limp clumps; her fingernails were painted a dark blue that matched her eye shadow. Lauren couldn't see the boy's face, but vinyl glitter and the words *Heavy Metal* sprawled across the back of his T-shirt. Lauren's mother would have killed her if she'd gushed like that in a public place, but still, she thought, they look happy.

"As long as we're changing the subject," she said as she pulled crust off the garlic bread, "that day at the Blooms"—she drew in a breath, then continued—"you were going to tell me what's been bothering you."

Staring past Lauren through smoke-dulled windows, Janaan remained silent.

"What is it?" Lauren pressed.

"Nothing. This just isn't the time. . . ."

"Sure it is. Look, you've dragged me out here, and I want to talk about someone other than me. That leaves you."

Shaking her head, Janaan said, "I'm not about to add to your problems."

"Then it's something I did."

"No!"

"Getting my mind off my problems and onto yours really would help me. I'm in the mood to listen. See those two over there?" she asked, jerking her head toward the couple. "They're sharing a single straw, wiping with the same napkin. They're even gnawing on the same piece of pizza! Can't you share one tiny problem with me?"

Janaan didn't smile. "I'm having trouble with my dad. Okay? Can we drop it now?"

So we're back to this again, Lauren thought. A great friend as long as it's on Janaan's terms. Something she was hiding needed to be said. Lauren leaned into the table and forced Janaan to meet her eyes.

"Don't shut me out, Janny. It isn't fair. Whatever it is, you can tell me. Your dad isn't on the college thing again? You can go, can't you?"

"My mom said I'll be there, no matter what. It's just . . ." She hesitated.

"What?"

"I don't know—you wouldn't understand. Your family's so disgustingly normal."

"We have our rough spots."

Janaan snorted.

"What is it! If it isn't school . . ."

"Okay, I'll tell you," Janaan broke in. "Have you ever heard of the Arab Political Action Group?"

"No."

"It's called APAG. They're a bunch of extremists from the Middle East living in this country. They do a lot of lobbying in Washington for Arab and oil rights. They're bizarre, Laurie. They hate everything American."

Indignant, Lauren said, "Then they should go back to the Middle East. Anyone who hates America should just leave it!"

"Fine. Except the 'they' now includes my father. He's one of them. He joined right after Adam died, and my life's been hell ever since."

Lauren exhaled slowly. "So . . . does he want you to join or something?"

"Join?" Janaan laughed harshly. "I hardly think so. Don't you know that Middle East women come somewhere between cattle and cattle droppings? No, he doesn't want me to join anything. He wants me to wear a veil and bow toward Mecca—to forget college and become an obedient wife to some Arab chauvinist. And I'm sick of it!" Color flamed across Janaan's cheeks; her eyes glittered. Now that she'd started, her words seemed to tumble, one after the other, like rocks down a slide. "He won't let me listen to the radio anymore— too many nasty lyrics. He monitors the television set so we won't see s-e-x on the tube, and then he insinuates that I am copulating with anything in pants."

"I can't believe he'd say that!" Lauren protested. "You hardly even date . . ."

Janaan's jaw tightened. "Don't tell me what my dad would or would not say. You weren't there! You don't know anything about my dad or my life!"

Hurt, Lauren said, "I'm your best friend. I think I know a thing or two about you."

"Well, then, you should know I don't lie. And I don't like you taking my dad's side!"

"I am not defending your father! How can you twist one comment into that? You want the truth? I wouldn't take your dad's side in a million years. I don't even like him. I've never liked the way he's treated you."

Janaan narrowed her eyes. "What's that supposed to mean?"

Lauren felt her face grow warm. She'd meant it as a show of support, but she could tell Janaan hadn't taken it that way. "I don't know—it just seems like he favors your brothers. That's not the point, though." She floundered. "Did your dad accuse you outright of having sex? Sometimes you read into things."

Tossing her pizza on the table, Janaan held up her hand, pointing to her fingers one by one. "You're a real friend, Lauren. Let's see, first, you think I'm too stupid to understand my own father. Next, you inform me my family isn't as good as your family—my dad doesn't treat me as well as your father treats you. And last but not least, you tell me I read more into things than you do. Now that's a real joke!" Janaan said in voice heavy with sarcasm. "I have never in my life seen anyone as hysterical as you are. Let's not forget the picture! I'm surprised you haven't brought that one up yet. I scribble on *my own* picture, you find it in *my things,* and then you grill me about it every chance you get!"

As she spoke her voice became louder and louder. Lauren looked around uncomfortably, then leaned forward and hissed, "Keep it down, Janny! People are listening!"

"I don't care! Let them!"

Lauren's fingers pressed hard against the tabletop. "What is with you tonight? We were having a simple conversation and suddenly you're attacking me. You're twisting my words so much I can hardly recognize them! I never said your dad doesn't treat you as well as my dad treats me. I did not even mention the picture. I think you're projecting your own feelings into our conversation. . . ."

"Oh, please, not the psychology." Janaan groaned. "You've taken two classes in high school and you want to set up shop. *Projecting*—I love it."

"Call it whatever you want." Lauren heard her own voice edge toward harshness. "Now I've got another word for you. *Asinine.* As in, you are acting like an ass."

Rolling her eyes toward the ceiling, Janaan shot back, "I'm sure you're right—you're always right. Blond-haired, blue-eyed Laurie, just this side of perfect in every way."

"Oh, that makes sense. Now you're accusing me of being blond. Is that why you ruined that picture, because you didn't like my coloring?"

"I destroyed that picture," Janaan said through clenched teeth, "because I am sick of you and your entire cute-as-pie family."

Lauren stared. The pizza lay cold and uneaten between them. "I know what your problem is," she said slowly. "You're jealous. I would never have believed it, but you're actually jealous of me."

"You don't know what I am. But let me tell you something, at least I do something about my problems. You fold up and die while the rest of the world has to go on. Look at me, I've got a dead brother, a father who's become a raving zealot, a mother who tells me she might get a divorce . . ."

"A divorce?"

"Yes. A divorce. My dad blames my mom for being gone when Adam died, and that started a lot of trouble between them. So you see, life for me isn't the party it is for you. Maybe I'm just tired of watching you have it all."

Before Lauren could say a word, a middle-aged woman swooped on their table. Squeezed into a tight peasant dress, she bent over their table, her breasts bulging in fleshy mounds. She smiled, and her eyes disappeared into plump, magenta cheeks.

"Would you kids like some more water?" she asked, grabbing and filling Lauren's glass before she had a chance to answer.

Lauren shook her head no.

"Um-hmmm. How about you, honey?" she asked as ice and water splashed into Janaan's glass.

Janaan didn't answer. The woman looked from one to the other, then quickly turned away. "Okay. If you need anything else, just let me know."

Reaching under her chair, Janaan grabbed her purse.

"I brought you here to cheer you up. I'm sorry this happened, but you had to push it. Let's go."

The metal chair-legs screeched against the floor as they were pushed back from the table. By the time Lauren collected her own purse and her sweater, Janaan had disappeared.

When Lauren reached the car, she found Janaan sitting stiffly behind the steering wheel. "You could have waited," she muttered as she slipped into her seat.

Janaan started the engine.

"Oh, the silent treatment. Great!"

As the car backed out, Lauren replayed the conversation. What had happened? It was like starting with a water lily, all beautiful on the outside, and then suddenly flipping it over to the gunk and ooze underneath. Tonight she'd seen things in her friend that she hadn't known were there. Maybe Janaan was right. Maybe she didn't know her at all.

The Saab edged toward the street and stopped behind a Buick waiting to make a left turn. Reflections from Fred's pizza sign slid across the hood like liquid pools of light. As she rolled down her window, Lauren breathed the cool air that swept in, heavy with the smells of stale pizza and exhaust fumes. Horns honked in the distance, cars swished by, people's feet made rhythmic clips that echoed into the night just like always. But Lauren felt different. It seemed everything in her life was dying. First Adam, then Rachael, and now her friendship with Janaan. Lauren didn't know how to stop it. And right then, she didn't know if she wanted to.

Without looking at her directly she studied Janaan, whose face flashed in and out of the oncoming lights. Janny was strong, she'd always been, but she used her strength like a wall. For the first time Lauren realized that a wall kept things in as well as out.

When they reached Lauren's house, the car pulled sharply against the curb.

"I don't know what happened, Laurie," Janaan began, her voice suddenly soft. "Sometimes I just get so mad . . . but it isn't fair to take it out on you. I am sorry."

Lauren drew in a deep breath and said, "I just don't like it when you turn on me. You can't rip me to shreds and then expect me to act like it didn't happen."

"You're right. Again. As usual. Good-night, Laurie."

Lauren watched the Saab speed down her street, the taillights glaring like angry red eyes. Janaan never looked back.

8

The bell rang.

"Drat!" Lauren said under her breath, as a pile of brightly colored folders slid from her top locker shelf, cascading like a paper rainbow onto the hall floor. She was late. Her first day back since Rachael died and she was late for phys ed.

Since she and Janaan shared the same locker, Lauren had deliberately waited until the last possible minute to get her things, hoping to avoid a run-in. The whole weekend had gone by since their blowup at Fred's, and they still hadn't spoken a word to one another. It wasn't that she was angry with Janaan—she was hurt!

Janaan should have talked about her feelings, instead of hitting Lauren all at once with so much emotional garbage. And yet . . . how could she call herself a best friend and not have known how Janaan was hurting? If Janaan was guilty of not speaking, maybe Lauren had been just as guilty . . . of not really seeing.

She bit her lip, then looked warily up and down the hall, but there was no sign of Janaan.

Out of the corner of her eye she saw the heavy wooden gym door swing shut. Lauren groaned. She had cut it too close, and now she'd have to humiliate herself by walking into a room full of girls sitting at attention on the hardwood floor. She hated being late!

Quickly retrieving her folders and stuffing them haphazardly onto the shelf, Lauren turned to run. As soon as her hand let go, the folders spilled on her head and spun across the hall floor.

"Oh, I give up!" She felt like a toad as she squatted and hopped, grabbing folders and pencils, hoping against hope Ms. Greenley would be late for once. That was unlikely. Rumor had it Ms. Greenley had been trained by the Russians.

Rapid footsteps made Lauren look up.

"Oh, Laurie, I'm so glad I found you!" Janaan cried, gripping her arm tightly while pulling her to her feet. Janaan's hand felt cold and damp; her skin gleamed with perspiration. Her eyes darted from Lauren to search the empty hallway, her whole body taut.

"I have to talk to you! I can't believe what's happening!"

"What's wrong? Are you all right?"

"I can't tell you here—come with me to my car. Please!"

Lauren shoved the folders back into her locker, all thoughts of their split forgotten. Janaan needed her, and nothing else was important.

Questions whirled through Lauren's mind as they tiptoed down the deserted hallway, praying a teacher wouldn't suddenly appear to demand a pass. At the end of the corridor Janaan stopped, looked cautiously around the corner, then motioned Lauren to follow until they made their way unnoticed through a side door. The Saab was parked against the curb with the engine running, Janaan's key chain dangling from the ignition.

"Janny, someone could have stolen your car!"

"Just get in! And watch behind us. The police are looking for me."

"The police!"

"Would you get in? I'll explain on the way."

The tires squealed as Janaan pulled from the curb and raced to the parking lot exit.

"Speeding is the best way to attract a police officer. Slow down!" Lauren warned.

Janaan hit the brakes and the car cut back to the speed limit. She glanced at Lauren. "Sorry. Listen, I know I'm dragging you away from school, and we haven't even talked since the other night. I really appreciate this. I don't know what I would have done if you were still mad at me."

"Of course I'm not mad. I was going to call you after school and smooth things out," Lauren lied. "Now talk. Where are we going, and who's after you?"

"I already told you. The police!"

"You're serious? I thought maybe you were being dramatic. What happened?"

"I don't even believe it myself. I mean, it's like I'm talking about someone else instead of me. I was on my way to school when I realized I'd forgotten my science project, so I hurried back home to get it. I saw a car parked out front, and when I came inside I heard my mom arguing with a man. They used my name, so I knew it had something to do with me."

Janaan swerved to miss a street-cleaning machine swirling its big flat brushes against the curb. "I listened to find out what it was about. They didn't even know I was there."

"Well? What did the man say?"

"He kept saying the same things over and over again, and my mom was crying because . . . because—" Her voice broke. Janaan stared rigidly ahead, not looking at Lauren. "I can't believe that witch—to say something like that."

"Who? Your mom?"

"Not my mom!" Janaan took a deep breath. "Remember that woman, that Cathy with the SIDS Foundation? Remember how she was staring at me, and you thought she might know me? Well, apparently she went to the police with a pack of lies. The detective kept telling my mother that once a complaint is filed, they have to act on it. He kept asking about me and . . . Adam."

"What does Adam have to do with anything? He's been dead for six months! They don't think that you . . ."

"That's exactly what they think! They're trying to say I'm a murderer—that I killed three babies, starting with my own brother!"

Shock, utter shock, slammed against Lauren. Houses on the street seemed to squeeze together, the colors of the asphalt and brick and trees kaleidoscoping into red and green and gray.

"Put your head between your knees and take a deep breath before you pass out," Janaan instructed coldly. Her voice seemed to hover against the ceiling of the car. Lauren dropped her head and felt a rush of blood in her ears. Seconds later the dizziness passed.

"What are you fainting for? I'm the one they accused of murder. If anyone should pass out, it should be me."

"I'm sorry," Lauren said weakly. "It's just . . . I wasn't ready for what you said."

"Who'd be ready to hear that they're riding in a car with a psychopathic killer?"

"Stop it! Maybe you misunderstood the detective. Did you ever talk to him, or did you just eavesdrop?"

"Laurie, I heard what he said. He wanted to know about my mental state and if I was easily excited. They think I'm a killer!"

Gripping the armrest, Lauren gasped. "I don't understand any of this. Why would anyone think you would murder a baby? Haven't they heard of crib death? And who are the other two babies you supposedly killed?"

"The detective told my mom that no one would have thought of foul play when Adam died, or even when Rachael died."

"Rachael!"

"But this Cathy went to the police and told them she was sure I held her baby the same day he died. She thought they'd better check things out. He asked my mother if I'd been 'disturbed' lately."

"You held another baby the day it died?" A jolt of fear shot down Lauren's back. The thought of Janaan hurting a child was absurd, ridiculous, and yet . . . to have three little babies die the same day they were with her . . .

"Don't you dare look at me that way, Lauren," Janaan commanded, her voice ice. "Don't even let the thought pass through your mind. I would never hurt a baby."

"Of course not! I know you, Janny. But to think you were around another baby the day it died is really weird. No wonder they're checking it out."

Janaan yanked fingers through her hair, pulling black spikes from her ponytail. "I know it sounds like too much of a coincidence, even to me, and I'm the one they're accusing!"

To hide her shaking hands, Lauren slid them under her thighs. "Do you remember this other baby?"

"You know, that's what I've been concentrating on. I think I might remember one, about three months ago, that I saw in a grocery store. It was no big deal, so I don't know if he's the one they're talking about. He was dressed in a darling snow suit and he was really fair, like Adam, and I was standing behind him in the checkout line. He kept smiling at me, and he was such a cute little guy that I almost started to cry. It'd only been three months since Adam died and this baby was so much like him. . . ."

"Do you remember the mother? I mean, was it Cathy?"

"I don't know," Janaan wailed. "I just don't remember. I wasn't looking at her, I was looking at the baby! He was reaching for me, so I asked if I could hold him just for a minute and his mom said sure, as long as I didn't have a cold. So I picked him up and hugged him, and then I put him back into the cart. I don't see how anyone could make something out of that!"

"No one could." Lauren patted Janaan's leg. "We both need to calm down—the whole thing has been blown way out of proportion. Now tell me exactly what the police are going to do. Do they have a warrant out for you?"

"I don't think so. Right now they just want to talk to me."

"Well, that's not so bad!"

"Except I haven't told you everything." She shot a glance at Lauren. "You don't know where we're going."

Lauren looked around her. She'd been concentrating so hard on what Janaan was saying she'd almost forgotten they were heading south, winding along back roads toward the foothills. Nothing was out here except older homes, a few small businesses clustered along the main street, and—Lauren gasped—the cemetery!

Janaan's green eyes narrowed and her jaw tensed. "They have a court order. He gave the papers to my mother. Due to the suspicious nature of the three deaths, they are exhuming my brother's grave."

"They've got no right!" Lauren cried. "It's sick! Oh, Janny, I'm sorry."

"I know his spirit isn't there. I know it's just his body, but it seems so wrong to open that tiny casket and take him out." She gripped the wheel so tightly her knuckles jutted white. "I keep thinking of some doctor cutting into what's left. . . ."

"Don't! You can't let yourself think that way. Are you sure they're going to do this?"

"Of course I'm sure."

"When?"

Janaan looked at her watch. "In about twenty minutes. That's why I had to bring you," she said, pulling into the parking lot of a small, sagging restaurant less than a block from the cemetery. "I've got to stay in the car so no one sees me. An order might be out to pick me up."

Trying to keep her voice steady, Lauren asked, "Why do you need me? I want to help, but I don't know what I can do."

Janaan turned in the seat to face Lauren. Her eyes were desperate. "I want you to be there when they exhume my brother. I want you to look at everything they do, listen to everything they say, then come back here and tell me."

9

Granite tombstones jutted from the hill like broken teeth. The old part of the cemetery was crowded with carved spires and stone angels trumpeting toward heaven. They towered over the newer graves, which were uniformly marked with plain square stones set flat into the ground. When Lauren had asked her mother why people didn't put up those beautiful statues anymore, her mother had explained that flat markers were now the rule, allowing a caretaker to mow right over the tops of the graves.

Inside the wrought-iron gates, two police cars were parked. Further up the hill, near Adam's grave, sat a van with the words *MEDICAL EXAMINER* painted on one side. An area twenty feet square had been cordoned off around the grave, where a group of men stood talking as they watched a caretaker shovel earth. Lauren hadn't counted on that. How was she supposed to get close? They'd wonder why she was there.

While the shovel bit deeper into the earth, Lauren stood at the gate. What could she tell them? That she was a reporter from the *Tribune* and had heard about what they were doing? She studied the men. No way would they believe she was old enough. She had on a pink cotton jumpsuit with rainbow hairclips—hardly the professional woman's attire. She chewed the corner of her lip and thought.

It would take guts to waltz up and lift those ropes, but who could stop her? Hoping her nerve would hold out, Lauren squared her shoulders and began to walk up the hill. One of the officers stopped talking to move toward her, breaking apart the cluster of men. They turned one by one to watch her pick her way through the tombstones.

"Hey, miss, you can't come in here. This is police business," a short officer with a thick middle and ruddy skin yelled, and motioned her away. Lauren looked down at the grass and kept walking.

"I'm sorry, miss, this area is roped off. You can't come through."

"But I've come to locate a relative's grave. I'm not from here and I've only got an hour—I'm researching my roots," she added weakly.

"I'm afraid you'll have to go. We're almost done here and then you can visit in peace."

"Can I wait here until you're finished?" Lauren asked, flashing a demure smile that seemed to fluster the officer.

"Honey, you don't want to watch this. We're pulling up a casket, and a pretty girl like you doesn't need to see a thing like that."

Lauren's smile faded. She deserved to be treated like a child when she'd tried to act cute instead of determined. "I'll wait," she said firmly.

The officer shrugged and muttered, "Suit yourself," as he rejoined the others near the grave.

She strained against the rope and watched the men dig. Sprays of earth were flung into soft brown drifts. In only minutes, a shovel blade scraped Adam's coffin lid. The sound made Lauren cringe.

"Okay, pull it up," the short officer ordered. The coffin was so small they lifted it easily onto the ground.

"This thing sure feels light," a workman commented. "You want to check it here, Mr. McCreary?"

A man wearing a suit, who might have been the coroner, approached the casket. "I think it would be a good idea. Let's make this official. Clem, come watch so it will be legal."

Lauren heard the squeak of a hinge, but she couldn't see anything. They'd formed a small semicircle around the casket to purposely shield her from their work.

"I'm opening the lid—oh my God!"

The men drew a collective breath as they leaned forward.

"Look at this!"

"I'll be . . . !"

Lauren couldn't stand it. She jerked up the rope and swung under it, then ran to Adam's coffin so quickly no one had time to stop her. What she saw made her blood freeze.

The casket was empty.

"In all my years, this is the . . . Who in God's name would steal the body of a little baby?" asked the officer.

Sun shimmered off the blue satin liner. The tufts and folds, smooth and untouched, looked perfect, as though time had stopped inside the dark earth.

Lauren backed away blindly, bumping the rope, then slipped under it to hurry toward the cemetery gate.

"Where's that girl going? Do you think she knows something about this?"

"Miss—you in the jumpsuit—I'd like to talk to you."

No! She couldn't talk to anyone. She had to think, to let her mind comprehend what she'd seen. What had happened to Adam? She pictured Janaan begging her to witness the unearthing of Adam's casket. . . .

"Hey, wait a minute! I want to talk to you."

"Sorry," Lauren called over her shoulder. Her voice sounded as though it belonged to someone else, to an imposter inhabiting her body.

"Stop!"

"Sorry."

She started to run. Her mind reeled. What was going on? Where was Adam's body? Could Janaan have had something to do with it? Stop—don't think that way— she's the best friend you've ever had. You know Janaan—she would never hurt anybody!

Her molars jarred as she ran, feet pounding on the concrete driveway, through the gate and onto the sidewalk that bordered the cemetery. Keep going, don't think. Her purse bounced against her hip. She could hear her own breathing as she approached the Saab, still parked in the corner of the lot. The passenger door swung open, and Janaan frantically motioned her inside.

"I thought you'd never get here. What happened—did anyone see you? Did you find out anything? What's wrong? Why are you looking at me like that—I can't stand this! Talk!"

"Adam's body, it . . ." Her voice faltered.

"It what? What happened?"

"They opened the casket, but Adam wasn't there. It was empty, Janaan. It was empty."

Color drained from Janaan's face as she fell back into her seat. Enraged, she had seemed charged with energy, larger than herself, but now she looked as small and limp as a rag doll.

"I don't believe you."

"It's true. I saw it. The coroner lifted the lid and nothing was there."

"Then they opened the wrong grave."

"It was his casket—they're not stupid. There's no mistake."

A tapping sound made them both jump. Two police officers flanked their car, signaling them with a metal club that rattled the window pane.

"Police officers. Are you Janaan Kashad?"

Janaan nodded slowly.

"Get out of the car. We want to question you on the death of your brother Adam Kashad. You have the right to remain silent."

10

The clacking sound of a typewriter rapped through the thin walls where Lauren sat, its monotonous rhythm broken by the occasional slam of a file drawer or by muffled laughter. She studied the worn carpet, the ceiling, the light fixture sprinkled with a layer of dead bugs, the bare walls—and waited. Years before, the room had been lime colored, but smoke and grime had darkened the paint to a bilious green. Lauren sat at a long wood-grained table, on a folding chair scratched down to the metal. Except for three other chairs and a clock, the room was empty.

Drumming her fingers nervously, she glanced again at the clock and replayed the last two hours of her life. She and Janaan had been kept apart from the start. The officers had separated them in the parking lot—to keep them from conspiring, Lauren supposed.

"She didn't do anything! Janaan loved her brother! At least let me ride in the car with her!" she had pleaded with the officer who led Janaan to his patrol car.

"I'm sorry, miss, she has to go alone. We'll be asking

you a few questions, but understand you are not being charged with anything."

"Where are you taking me? Do I have to go to the police station?"

The other officer motioned Lauren to get into the backseat of a second patrol car. He was young, maybe five years older than she, but he spoke to her like a father to an errant child.

"You don't have to come, but if we need to we can get a warrant."

"Is Janaan being arrested?"

"I don't know. But if you go with me to the station, I'm sure I can find out. It's only a couple of questions." He smiled. "Can we count on your help?"

"When can I see her?"

"I can't promise anything, but your chances will be a lot better if you cooperate. Okay?"

She had nodded yes, then later found herself shuffled from one set of people to the next until she was led to the green room. And then she'd waited. Every time she heard the sound of approaching footsteps her stomach squeezed, but no one came in. She could hear the click of the wall clock's second hand, the murmur of voices, and the distant ring of a telephone. An hour crept by. I'll just leave, she told herself, but she didn't move. More footsteps, and finally the door swung open and three men entered.

The first was short and squatty, with features that reminded Lauren of a lump of dough. A soft ball for a chin, a bulbous nose—even his eyes were draped with fleshy lids.

"Are you Lauren Taylor?" he asked, pulling one of the folding chairs from the table. "This is Detective Michaelson and you already know Officer Shupe. I'm Detective Bentner. We're sorry to keep you waiting so long, but we wanted to talk to Janaan first before we came to you. Do you mind if I smoke?"

Without waiting for an answer, he pulled a pack of cigarettes from his shirt pocket. "I need to quit, but every time I do I head straight for the vending machine down the hall. By the way, can I get you anything? Candy? A Coke?"

"No, thank you. Where's Janaan?"

Detective Bentner scooted closer to Lauren. Officer Shupe dropped into one of the chairs, while Detective Michaelson perched on the edge of the table.

"Before we get started, I want to make it clear that you personally are not under suspicion. Do you understand? We just want to talk with you to clear up a few things."

"I understand. What's happening—how's Janaan?"

"She's fine. She's in another room just like this one. Now before we go on, I'd like to ask your permission to tape your comments. Taping is just an aid for us— sometimes Detective Michaelson takes terrible notes. Is that all right with you?"

"I don't care, just as long as you stop talking to me like I've had a lobotomy and tell me what's going on!"

The smile faded from the detective's face. He lit his cigarette, inhaled deeply, then blew two streams of smoke from his nostrils.

"What's going on is your friend's been around three kids that are dead, one of which is now both dead and missing. Now suppose you tell me what you know about Janaan, starting with the way she felt about her brother."

The tape recorder clicked on. Lauren looked at the circle of faces, at the men staring like cats ready to pounce. "She loved her brother. I mean, what can I say? She adored him. She loved—loves all babies."

"Did she ever express any jealousy toward Adam?" Detective Michaelson asked, moving closer.

"No! She loved him!"

"Never? She never said she was tired of baby-sitting him? She never said that?"

"I don't remember specifics, but I do know that she loved him."

"Did she ever say she wanted to go somewhere but couldn't because she had to watch the baby?" Officer Shupe began.

"Maybe, but so what?"

"How does she feel about her father? How do they get along?" Detective Bentner interrupted.

Lauren looked at her hands. She needed to compose herself, to slow down. They asked questions before she had a chance to really think.

"You're hesitating. Remember, Lauren, the truth can't hurt her. How would you characterize the relationship between Janaan and her father? Is it warm and loving? We already know what she said, but we want to hear from you."

"All we want to know is what you think," Detective Michaelson added.

"I think," Lauren said slowly, "that this has nothing to do with the fact that some babies died of crib death. I think you're trying to say Janaan hurt someone, when she didn't. And I think it stinks."

"All right, Lauren," Detective Bentner said, taking another drag from his cigarette. "We know you're her friend, so you don't have to prove anything. Now answer the question. How do Janaan and her father get along? And cut the crap."

"Hey, Bentner, lighten up," Michaelson broke in. "This has been pretty hard on her, too. She's not playing games, are you, Laurie?"

Detective Michaelson was fortyish, lean, and homely in what Lauren thought was a nice sort of way. His smile gave her courage to go on.

"Janaan and her father have had a few problems. He's pretty strict with her, but she really loves him. Okay?"

"Everybody just loves everybody—is that it?" Bentner asked.

"Yes, that's it."

"Has he treated her the same way he's treated the other kids in the family?"

Lauren could feel herself color. "I don't know."

"Come on, Lauren, tell us the truth. Does he treat her

the same as the boys in the family? Did he treat her the same way as Adam?"

"I said I don't know!" Lauren shouted. "What is it with you? Ask Janaan about her dad because I just don't know!"

"Back off, Bentner," Michaelson warned.

"Hey! I'm asking the questions. We've got a possible murder on our hands, maybe three of them. For all we know this one's in on it." He turned to Lauren and narrowed his eyes. "This is a damn picnic compared to what'll happen if this thing goes to trial. Now I asked a straight question and I want a straight answer. Has the dad been treating all the kids the same or not?"

"Go to hell."

Her hands were shaking, and her voice quivered like a reed. She'd never in her life talked to an adult that way, let alone a middle-aged detective. But she wasn't going to let herself get pushed into saying things that could hurt Janaan. No one could make her do that.

"Officer Shupe, you said I didn't have to be here. Well, I don't want to do this anymore. Can I leave now?"

"You can if you insist, but it'll just make things harder in the long run. . . ."

"I don't care about the long run. I want to go home."

Detective Michaelson slid off the table and stood behind her. He rested a strong hand on her shoulder and faced Bentner.

"Why don't you get out of here and let me talk with

her? Would that be okay with you, Laurie? Just a few more questions, and then I'll take you home myself."

When she hesitated, he flashed another smile and added, "I'll try to get you in to see Janaan, if that'll help."

Lauren looked from his smiling face to Bentner's glowering expression. "I can see Janaan?"

"If it's at all possible."

"Will we be . . . will Detective Bentner have to be here?"

"Not if you don't want him to."

"Wait a minute!" Bentner broke in angrily.

"Shut up, Bentner. Go get a cup of coffee. Well, Laurie?"

"All right. What do you want to know?"

"Take a powder," Michaelson ordered Bentner.

Without looking at either of them, Detective Bentner jumped to his feet and slammed the door behind him.

"Officer Shupe, could you run down to the machine and get Laurie a soft drink and a doughnut?"

"I'm not . . ." she began.

"It's okay. If you don't want them, the department can absorb the loss. I'd just as soon have something to munch on while we talk. I'll take a sugar doughnut—in fact, bring a couple."

"Sure," Shupe said, scurrying out the door.

Michaelson smiled at Lauren. "They don't taste as stale as the rest. So, how old are you? Nineteen?"

"No, I'm a senior, like Janaan. I'm seventeen. I'll be eighteen in June."

"I've got a daughter just about your age. She's in pep club. You in anything like that?"

Lauren shook her head.

"I'm surprised—you're just the type. All that blond hair. I could have sworn you'd be out there swinging pom-poms around. Are you active in sports?"

"Not much. Look, I'd really like to get on with this."

He cleared his throat, then slipped into the chair vacated by Bentner.

"Laurie, I want you to know something. Even though we've known each other such a short while, I have a good feeling about you. I can tell you have a real instinct about people. That Bentner can be an ass. He's been on the job too long. I don't know how to put it into words—he's kind of hard when it comes to people. He sees the worst in them."

Michaelson leaned forward and clasped his hands between his knees. "But I'm more like you. When I build a relationship with someone, I feel I know them, almost the way I know myself. That's the part I want you to tell me about Janaan. Everything you can think of, no matter how small or insignificant you might think it is, I want you to tell me. It's the best way you can help her."

"Well, for starters I know she couldn't hurt anyone. It would be totally out of her nature."

"Good. That's a good start. Why do you think it would be out of her nature? Is she the type of person that never gets angry, the type that just bottles everything up inside?"

"Well . . . she's sort of a bubbly type, hardly ever down."

"So when she's upset, you'd hardly know it because she keeps it in?"

"Right. She's a very 'up' person."

"Does Janaan tell you everything, or is she closer to someone else—say a boyfriend?"

"Oh, no, I'm the closest one to her. We share just about everything."

"What about a boyfriend? Does she have one?"

"Not really," Lauren said, relaxing. Detective Michaelson kept looking at her in such a friendly way; she could feel his support stealing over her. "Her dad gives her such a hard time whenever she tries to go out that she's just sort of quit trying. Like I said, he's really strict."

"But Janaan didn't let that get to her. She probably thought, 'Well, college is just around the corner, so it's not a big deal to wait until then.' "

"Well, yes and no. There were times when I think she wanted to kick a wall or two, but she was mostly okay."

Officer Shupe appeared with cans of Coke and Slice and a plate holding three doughnuts balanced on top of the cans. Lauren took the Slice and opened it. She was thirsty after all.

"Did she tell you she wanted to kick the wall, or did you just know her well enough to see that she was bothered?"

"I just knew her well enough. I don't see what any of this has to do with Adam."

Michaelson grabbed a doughnut and took a bite. "Not much. I'm just trying to find out how well you know her, the deep-down stuff she might have been thinking."

"Nobody's closer to her than I am."

"I believe you." He smiled again. "You probably know her better than her own father."

"No kidding." Lauren snorted.

"I guess from what Janaan said, they haven't been getting along too well. He favored Adam, didn't he? How did that make her feel?"

"Oh, she noticed it, all right. I mean, it would have been hard not to. But she never really talked about it. I don't think she lost any sleep over it."

"It was one of those problems she sort of buried inside."

Lauren nodded. "Yeah, I think it was. But it didn't stop her from loving Adam."

"She was like a mother to him, wasn't she, because her parents were involved with their own problems?"

"Uh-huh, except the problems didn't get really bad until after Adam died. Her dad blamed her mother. He was really crazy about Adam."

"It's funny that Mr. Kashad didn't blame Janaan. Wasn't she the one baby-sitting when Adam died?"

Lauren's brows knit together. "You're right. You'd think Mr. Kashad would have been madder at Janaan. But she told me he was angry at her mom. Definitely. I remember she said that."

The chair squeaked as Michaelson leaned into it. "Boy, it sounds like she's been living in a pressure cooker. No dating, a death in the family, problems between her parents—it's a good thing she's had you for a friend. You must have held her hand a lot. Did Adam look like Janaan?"

"No. In fact, unless you knew better, you'd swear they weren't brother and sister. He was really blond—wait—I think I have a picture of the two of them together."

She bent underneath her chair and retrieved her purse, laying it on the table in front of the two of them. "Let me see," she said, taking out her wallet and shuffling through the plastic inserts. "Here it is; I thought I still had this one. See, there's Janaan trying to get Adam to drink his bottle. He doesn't have much hair, but still you can tell how fair he is."

Detective Michaelson's eyes slid over the photograph and rested on Lauren's open purse. The dog-eared corner of a photograph edged out from beneath her pack of tissues.

"What's this?" he asked, pulling the picture from her purse.

Lauren's breath caught in her throat. He'd found—no, taken—the photograph Janaan had defaced. How could he just grab something from her purse, as though he had every right to!

"Give that to me!" Lauren shouted, reaching for the picture.

It was too late. Detective Michaelson spun himself so his back was toward her, and extended the photograph out of her reach.

"Looks like someone was pretty unhappy. Janaan did this, didn't she?"

Lauren didn't answer. Her brain felt congealed with jumbled thoughts. One thing exploded at her—Michaelson had tricked her! He'd just been trying to milk her for information about Janaan, and now he had something devastating.

"You aren't the type, Lauren. I can tell Janaan did this. She was angry with you, angry with the world."

"I did that," Lauren said coldly. "It's my picture. I'm only seventeen, but I know something about the law. You can't go through my things without asking permission." She leaned across the table so that her mouth was only inches from the tape recorder. "Put it back in my purse or I swear to God I'll call the American Civil Liberties Union."

Slowly Michaelson's hand came down. He looked at Lauren, then tossed the picture onto the table.

"I can't figure why a girl like you would try to cover for a girl like that. She could be a killer! A baby killer!"

Lauren pushed her chair from the table and stood up. "I came here to help you, but I can tell you've already made up your mind about Janaan. You think she did it?" Her voice was clear, hard. "Well, Detective, show me the evidence! You're ready to hang Janaan, and you've got nothing. Nothing! Let me tell you and your tape recorder: I believe in Janaan." She spun around and headed for the door. "As far as I'm concerned, this interview is over."

At that moment, Detective Bentner hurried into the room and handed Michaelson a paper.

The lines that etched Michaelson's face deepened as though they'd been carved with a knife. Quickly he scanned the paper a second time.

"You're sure?"

"Of course I'm sure, I just talked with the guys. This thing is weird."

"What thing?" Lauren searched Bentner's face. "What did you find out?"

Michaelson and Bentner exchanged glances. "Might as well tell her," Bentner said flatly. "Maybe she'll help us if she knows the truth."

Michaelson stared at the paper, then at Lauren.

"Okay, sure, I'll tell you. Seems like your little friend's been busy. They've just exhumed the graves of Rachael Bloom and Kevin Meyer. And guess what they found? Nothing. Just two more empty little coffins."

He got up slowly and walked toward Lauren. "Janaan was with three babies. Three babies died. And now," he said, leaning closer, "their bodies are missing. You want evidence, Lauren?" His mouth was only inches away, so close she could smell his breath as he whispered, "Go look in the caskets."

11

Lauren paced across her bedroom floor, stopping every few minutes to peer impatiently out her window. Petals from her lavender azalea plant curled on her window ledge, like tiny scraps of dried velvet. She picked up a dried petal, as delicate as an insect wing, and crumbled it to dust between her fingers as she searched the street for Janaan's car.

Where was she? An hour had crawled by since Lauren had answered the phone and heard Janaan's clipped voice.

"Laurie, we need to talk. I'll be over in ten minutes."

"Are you okay? It's been almost two days and I haven't heard a word from anyone. Your folks won't even answer the phone and my parents—"

"I can't talk now," Janaan had interrupted. "I've got to go. Just be there."

A click and then a dial tone. Lauren had been cut off. She'd felt cut off from everyone since Detective Michaelson had turned off the tape recorder and let her leave the tiny box of an office.

A uniformed officer, a husky man with skin the color of coffee, had been assigned to drive her home. As he punched the elevator button for the parking garage, he'd said, "You got any ideas what happened to those babies?"

"Who told you to ask? Bentner? Or Michaelson?"

During the elevator ride, he hadn't answered. When the door slipped open, he'd nodded for her to precede him, and as she'd passed, he'd muttered, "Bentner."

They'd begun the drive to her home in silence. From the backseat of the car, Lauren had seen packs of kids racing through sprinklers and sucking Popsicles in their effort to cool off in the ninety degree heat. The sun beat onto the sidewalks, glinted off windows, stifled the air. Her mother had been called before Lauren left the station and would be there, waiting, when Lauren got home.

Pressing her forehead against the window of the squad car, she'd felt its coolness; it was cool and clear and hard. That glass separated her from the hot air outside, and in a strange way from life on the other side. An elderly couple rested on a porch swing, a little girl skated down her driveway—life for them went on just as always. If only Lauren could have stopped the car and joined them. If only she could forget what she'd seen, what she knew, and just be like everyone else.

She'd turned toward the officer, who'd been glancing at her in the rearview mirror. "Excuse me, what time is it?" she'd asked. "I've totally lost track of time."

"Twenty after three."

She'd fallen back into the seat and pushed sweaty bangs off her forehead.

"I heard what they said about your friend," he'd begun. "Must be rough. Real rough." The top of his hat skimmed against the car ceiling as he talked. When he glanced at her over his shoulder, his eyes had seemed kind. "That girl—what's your friend's name again?"

"Janaan."

"Right. Janaan. I thought you'd like to know that her mama's there with her. But don't count on her getting out just yet."

"Why not?" she'd asked, snapping to attention. "Has she been charged with anything?"

The officer shrugged. "No. But they got a lot more questions since those other babies turned up gone. I'd say your friend won't be out till tonight, if she gets out at all."

"I can't believe this!" Lauren had exploded. "It's not fair!"

In a voice dropped low, he said, "What happened to those little babies doesn't seem fair, either."

Lauren returned her gaze to the outside. What is it with these people, she'd thought fiercely. Haven't they heard of innocent until proven guilty? "You already believe she's guilty, don't you?" she'd asked. "Just like everybody else."

"Is that what you think?"

She'd nodded. "Yeah, it is."

"Well," the officer said, his voice mild, "then you think wrong. By the way, I never introduced myself. My name is Tyson. Jake Tyson." He'd reached a broad hand across the back of the seat.

"Hi." Lauren shook his hand. "You're the first person I've talked to that believes Janaan is innocent."

"I don't know if she is."

"But you just said . . ."

"I've never even met the girl. I've seen the paper on her, but I never had the chance to talk with her, so I just don't know. With me, it all boils down to my gut." He pointed through the windshield and asked, "Is that your house up ahead?"

"Yes. The brick one. Listen, I don't get what you're saying. Do you believe her or not?"

Tyson exhaled slowly. "Well, I've heard the word around the station. They all figure your friend's a killer." He'd parked in her driveway and turned to look at her. "Me, I have no opinion whatsoever. I see a couple of tough-guy detectives solving a case the first day they get it. Maybe they're right, maybe they're wrong. My advice to you, before you get in any deeper, is to ask your own gut which is which."

"That's easy," she'd declared. "Janaan's innocent."

"Well, then, that's fine. Fine. So far you've been real loyal in defending your friend. You just listen if your insides tell you any different." His smile crinkled the corners of his eyes. "There's your mama coming, so I'll say good-bye now. Good luck to you, Lauren."

The squad car had barely pulled away before she felt the crush of her mother's arms. "Oh, honey, you should have called me the instant they took you to the police station," Marilyn cried. "Are you all right?" She'd held Lauren's face between her hands and searched her eyes. "They had no right to keep you there. Your father is in a rage—he left work the second he heard and he's inside waiting for you now."

She'd hugged her again, hard, and Lauren noticed how soft her mother's body had become. Gray-white hair, scented with traces of herbal shampoo, brushed her cheek. The endless day was finally over. She was home.

They had talked until Lauren was exhausted. Her parents seemed to believe in Janaan, but she sensed their doubt. When she'd pressed to see Janaan, her father had said, "We shouldn't rush things. Let's give the legal system a chance. Although I have half a mind to sue the whole police department. Janaan's eighteen, but you're still a minor. Imagine! Holding a juvenile without informing the parents!"

"I told them I'd stay, Dad. They didn't force me. But that's not the point. Officer Tyson said she'd be out tonight, and I want to be there. They won't tell me anything over the phone. I've got to go!"

Her mother's hand had reached to cover Lauren's. "Sweetheart, you've been through a lot. We're very worried about Janaan, but right now our main concern is you. How about the three of us going out to eat, then we'll come back and put you to bed."

"I'm not a child—I don't need tucking in. We can't

just desert Jan! She's innocent and you won't let me help her."

Lauren had seen her father's jaw set. His voice had been terse as he'd told her, "You are not responsible for what happens from this point on. You've already done more than you should have."

He'd leaned forward to spread his large fingers over their clasped hands. "Be careful, Laurie. You can't let yourself get dragged down, because it could be a long, long way."

The next two days had crept by without a word from Janaan or her family. The phone had silently taunted, refusing to ring no matter how hard Lauren willed it to. Finally the phone call; and then the wait for Janaan to arrive.

Lauren stared out the window at the peach tree, counting the hard pale fruit, when a movement at her doorway caught her eye. She whirled to face Janaan.

"Janny, you scared me to death! How'd you get in here?"

"I used the back. I hope you don't mind. Is anyone else home?"

Lauren shook her head no. Janaan must not have eaten or slept since Lauren last saw her. She looked like a living shadow. Hollows darkened her cheeks, the skin around her eyes was puffy and tinged with blue. An oversized white T-shirt hung carelessly over rumpled jeans, and, for the first time Lauren could remember, she wore no makeup.

"Laurie, it is so good to see you. I thought I'd never get out of that sewer," she said. "Did your parents know I was coming?"

"No, I didn't tell them. It's not what you think," she explained, catching Janaan's expression. "They believe in you totally. It's just that I wanted some time with you alone. So, how come the police released you?"

Narrowing her eyes, Janaan bit off every word. "Because I didn't do anything and they finally figured it out."

"You're not a suspect anymore?"

"I didn't say that! They don't have enough evidence to hold me any longer, that's all. I feel like I'm in a twilight zone or something. I've spent hours answering so many questions I'm not sure what my own name is. And that room was hideous. I'll tell you one thing, Laurie, I'll never be locked up again."

She collapsed on Lauren's bed, pulled her knees to her chin, and stared out the window. Lauren leaned against her wall and watched, her hands clasped together at the small of her back. For a moment, neither of them spoke. After all her anticipation, Lauren felt at a sudden loss for words.

Finally Janaan broke the silence. "I hated every second there," she said, her face grim. "They kept asking the same things over and over again, as though I'd break if they hammered me long enough."

"I know, they grilled me, too. I'm just glad you're

finally here. What took you so long, Janny? I was going crazy waiting for you. You said ten minutes!"

Janaan's eyes rested on the wilted azalea.

"You need to water your plant, Laurie. Look at it, it's dying right in front of you and you're not doing a thing to save it." She raised her eyes and said to Lauren, "I was talking to my father."

Ever since the nightmare had started, the thought of Abdul Kashad and Janaan together had frightened Lauren; Janaan's father seemed capable of anything. She crossed over and settled next to Janaan, then asked, "You want to talk about it?"

Without meeting her eyes, Janaan nodded. "My dad was out of state when they picked me up. He took the first flight back. Lauren, you don't know how scared I was, waiting for him to get home. I thought he was going to kill me. I thought he would believe *them.*" She looked away. "It was late when he got back. When he came in he just dropped his suitcase, and then"—her voice choked—"then he gave me a hug. He said he knew I was innocent."

Her voice faltering in surprise, Lauren said, "I'm glad."

"He said he would do everything he could to get me out of this mess. After the hug I must have looked as surprised as you do, because he said 'Janaan, don't you know that I love you?' And I just looked up at him and shook my head no."

"What happened?" Lauren asked.

"Well, he just sat for a long time—didn't say a word.

Finally he stood up and started pacing. I got a sick feeling in my stomach, because I thought he'd yell, but he didn't. He . . . he talked to me!"

Janaan jumped off the bed and walked to Lauren's dresser. "He said he thought Mom and I hated his country and its traditions, and that if we hated his country, it was the same as hating him."

As she talked she picked up, then set down, Lauren's collection of glass figurines, placing each piece in a precise line.

"What about your brothers? How come all this is just you and your mom?"

"I asked him that. He said that in his culture, a man's honor depends on the way his wife and daughters behave, and that I'm behaving too much like an American. I told him I thought I behaved just fine, that I've never done anything to shame him. Once I started I couldn't stop—I told him how angry I felt, how cut off from him I've always been. He said *I* was the one who'd pulled away."

Still touching the figurines, Janaan went on, "He said I always reject his ways, that my mom and I are the ones who refuse to bend. I told him, 'That's not true, I've always tried to do things the way you want, like not eating pork or not listening to the music I like.' And he said, 'Yes, but that's only when I'm around to police you. The minute I'm gone, you do what you please.' " She turned and looked at Lauren. "He's right."

"That's not a reason to freeze you out," Lauren objected. "Just because you chose something different."

"I know, but I've never thought of how he might see things. Funny how we live in the same house and think so differently."

Lauren twisted her hair into a knot, then let it drop onto her back. "Did he say what's going to happen with him and your mom?"

"Just that it was between the two of them, and that they'd work it out."

"Well, anyway," Lauren said, "he must be relieved that the police let you go. It's finally over."

Janaan stiffened.

"It's not that simple. I wasn't released because they believed me. I was released because the police didn't have enough evidence to hold me. As that jerk of a detective put it, they had reasonable suspicion but not probable cause. So here I am."

"Well, who cares why? The point is you haven't been charged. You need to forget it now, Janny. Like I said, it's over."

"Not by a long shot," Janaan said coolly. "You should have seen how they looked at me when I left the police station—they still think I did it. And let's face it, Laurie, even you aren't one hundred percent sure about me. Are you?"

It wasn't a question, but a statement of fact. They had always been able to read each other perfectly, sometimes too clearly. Lauren raised her eyes defiantly to meet Janaan's steady gaze.

"You're right, I did wonder."

"I knew it. . . ."

"Wait a minute, I'm not done. When they opened Adam's casket, I didn't know what to think. Yes, it crossed my mind. But then, well, it's like a certain officer told me, I had to go with my gut. I know you, Janny. Maybe not as well as I thought I did, but enough to know you couldn't hurt anyone. No matter what, I believe in you."

"Thanks," Janaan said softly. "That means a lot to me." She paused, then added, "But it's not enough. I can't stand to live with the stares, the whispers, 'Did you know every baby Janaan's around dies? And their bodies disappear?' They could never prove anything, but . . ." As her voice rose she slammed her fist into the dresser, making the figurines jump. "There's no evidence! No fingerprints, no blood, no witnesses, no bodies, nothing to send me to jail, but nothing to prove I'm innocent. It's up to us, Laurie. You've got to help me find out who killed my brother!"

12

They half walked, half ran across the glass-specked asphalt. Lauren felt Janaan tense as they approached the entryway of the police station, the building that had held Janaan through the long hours of questioning. Blue-uniformed men and women pushed in and out the double doors; it was four-thirty, time for many to go home and forget the grinding day. Maybe they're gone, Lauren worried. Maybe it's too late.

She and Janaan followed a maze of hallways until they reached Detective Michaelson's cramped office. The door was open; he sat behind a metal desk, the same kind Lauren's teachers used in school. Dragging on a cigarette, he talked brusquely into the phone. Stacks of folders and crumpled papers crowded his desktop to the edges, with only a small square cleared for writing. Lauren hung back, suddenly afraid to go in.

"Damn it, I'm not crazy. We're supposed to look at all the angles." He paused, then shouted, "I'm not suggesting you're incompetent; I'm asking a valid medical question." His brows knit when he saw Lauren and

Janaan. Motioning them inside, he barked, "I'll need to call you back, there's someone here. Thanks for all the help." He bit off the last word.

"Well, ladies, what brings you two here? I thought you couldn't wait to get away from us, Janaan."

"I—that is we—we forgot to tell you something," Janaan stuttered. "We think we might know who did all this."

Michaelson formed a bridge with the tips of his fingers and peered over them, scrutinizing Janaan and Lauren. They were an odd pair, he mused. The tall blond, Lauren, seemed nervous but controlled. Janaan, in contrast, looked as she had after tedious hours of questioning, hovering against the wall, nails dug into the bare skin of her arms. Her eyes darted around the room. From years of dissecting souls, Michaelson understood what lay behind those eyes. Fear.

"So, you've figured out who the culprit is. Is this a confession?"

"No!" Janaan said. Turning to Lauren, she snapped, "I told you we should have gone to someone else."

"Detective Michaelson, we're here to help. When Janaan and I finally got together, we realized neither one of us had mentioned something that happened the day Rachael died. Do you want to hear it or not?"

"I'm listening. Sit down."

Lauren pulled a chair from against the wall and placed it squarely in front of Michaelson as Janaan slid into a chair already facing him. The two paused, looked at each other, then at Michaelson's expectant face.

"The day Rachael died," Lauren began, "I had her outside for a walk. This lady—she said her name was Marjorie—came up and started talking to me. Well, Rachael crawled over to her and this Marjorie picked her up. She wouldn't give Rachael back to me. I tried everything, but she said she wanted Rachael for her own."

"Wait a minute, are you telling me Rachael was kidnapped? That's a hell of a thing to forget to mention."

"No—yes—I mean, she was for a little while. This Marjorie was crazy, talking about her baby, Irene, except Irene was just a doll. She was pushing it around in a baby carriage."

"Did Rachael's parents know about this?"

"The next time I saw them, Rachael was already dead. It didn't seem important at the time."

Michaelson opened his drawer and pulled out a notebook. "Did you say this woman's name was Marjorie?"

"That's what she told me."

"And she threatened Rachael?"

"No! But Rachael was screaming and I tried to get her to give Rachael to me and she wouldn't!"

"Oh, I see. She held on to a crying baby."

Lauren glanced at Janaan, but Janaan was staring at her hands.

"She looked wild, in the eyes," Lauren said hotly. "She wouldn't give her back. A man had to come help me. . . ."

"Where was Janaan?"

"She was inside—she didn't see anything."

"Who was this man? Was he a neighbor?"

"I don't know. He came across the street to help, but then another man showed up. I think he was Marjorie's husband. He was the one who handed Rachael back."

"Do you remember the husband's name?"

"No."

"Do you know the stranger's name?"

"No . . ."

"Did this Marjorie try in any way to hurt Rachael—say by grabbing her neck or putting her hand over her mouth?"

"Not exactly."

"What *exactly* did she do?"

"I already told you! She grabbed Rachael and refused to give her back."

"Did you call the police?"

"I wanted to, but Janaan didn't think we should."

Michaelson glanced at Janaan. "Oh? That's interesting. Why not, Janaan?"

Janaan cleared her throat. "I felt sorry for her."

There was a silence. Lauren tried to gather her thoughts, to get the conversation back on a straight line. "You haven't even asked me about the doll. She was pushing a doll around like it was a real baby." Lauren's voice rose. "Why are you trying to get Janaan? We came here to give you some information, but your mind is closed." She jumped out of her chair. "Let's go. He's not going to check into this."

"Listen, girls. . . ."

"No, you listen!" Lauren spun around to face him.

"No one is interested in the truth. You're just trying to find more nails to fit in Janaan's coffin." Oh, God, she thought, why did I use those words? "Never mind, we'll figure this out on our own!" She grabbed Janaan's arm and practically yanked her to her feet.

"Before you go, I want you to know something," Michaelson said. "We are detectives; we do this for a living. It may surprise you to know that we already checked out Marjorie Kensington. She's a little off the beaten path, I grant you, but her doctors say she's harmless. And by the way, if that doesn't convince you, try this—she was locked up in a psychiatric ward during the time Adam and Kevin died, and, except for your little incident, was in the constant care of Mr. Kensington the day Rachael died. So you see, Marjorie couldn't have done it." His dark eyes bore accusingly into Janaan's.

Janaan's gaze locked with his. Tension charged between the two of them until Lauren could almost see it. She realized Michaelson had been playing with them—again!—hoping something damning would slip.

Lauren stretched to her full five foot nine and glared down on him. "You," she said calmly, "are a cold-blooded manipulator." Taking Janaan by the arm, she propelled her out the door.

Water licked the pebbled shore of the lake in Sugarhouse Park. Sugar Lake was really a glorified pond, a man-made acre of water dug dead center in the park. Lauren and Janaan sat silently in the surrounding grass, watching as a family of ducks honked and shook their heads, spraying beads of water from their feathers like unstrung pearls.

"Well!" Janaan's cool voice broke into the silence. "That was a bust. I really thought we had something. And I love the way Michaelson works everything around to me. Must be a gift."

"The jerk," Lauren muttered. "We've learned something from him, anyway. We can't depend on anyone but ourselves."

Someone had left a few stale crusts from a sandwich on the grass nearby, and Lauren broke off a piece and tossed it into the water. Two baby ducks raced over, their necks craned toward the floating bread. The larger duck reached the bread first and gobbled the piece in one gulp.

"Here, see if you can throw this by the smaller one," Lauren said, handing a chunk of crust to Janaan. "The big duck steamrolled the little duck."

Janaan flung the piece, hitting the smaller duck on its bill. It quickly snapped up the offering and paddled away.

"An analogy of life, Laurie. The bigger you are, the more you get. Those detectives can steamroll us because we're small and they have all the power. The system stinks."

"Don't worry about Michaelson. He's got more experience, but we'll compensate. The two of us are smart, Janny. We are! The worst thing we can do is let him intimidate us."

Sighing, Janaan leaned back on her elbow. "I just feel that whatever we try to do, he'll get there first and roll right over us."

"Look, the only part of that analogy that fits is that Michaelson is a big duck! Okay?"

Janaan grinned. "Your jokes are getting as bad as mine. The thing is, I can't believe he already knew about Marjorie. Michaelson's gathering information to prove a theory, which is that I'm guilty." Rolling onto her stomach, she propped her chin in her hands and looked at Lauren. "I don't know what to do now. Any suggestions?"

"Well," Lauren began, "the way I see it, their biggest advantage is their access to information. They can pick up a phone and find out what the Meyer baby had for breakfast. We can't. The only thing we've got to work with is what we can remember. So I suggest we sit and brainstorm, write it all down, then check to see if there's any kind of pattern. Understand?"

"Barely. I think the distilled version is remember and write. You've got a great future in politics, Laurie."

"Thank you. I think. Anyway, before we start we need a pencil and paper. You got any?"

"Let me check." Janaan rifled through her purse. "Here we go. Okay, I'm ready. Now what?"

Staring out at the water, Lauren tried to visualize a way to begin. The murky water, glazed with a sheen of sunlight, spread fans of water tipped with gold. She was glad they had driven here after their encounter with

Michaelson. The lake had a calming effect, smoothing away her frustration.

"First of all, let's start with everything the babies had in common. We'll make three columns and see what we get."

"How about the fact that I was around every one of them the day they died?" Janaan bristled.

"Don't get so touchy. Actually, that's a very good thing. You were there, so you more than anyone will know what they had in common." Lauren rubbed her arm. "One person did it and took the bodies. If it wasn't Marjorie, it was somebody else. There has to be a reason he or she chose those three babies. For example, they were all approximately the same age. Six months. Write that down."

Janaan frowned, then drew in a breath. "I thought of something weird. They all looked the same. Did you notice? Three towheads with blue eyes."

"That's right! It could be a coincidence, but write it down. Okay, there were two boys and one girl, so the sex didn't seem to matter. What else?"

Hesitating, Janaan answered, "In two cases the parents weren't home, but Mrs. Meyer was home when her son died."

"So that's not the same." Lauren bit her lip in thought. "What time did Adam die?"

"I don't know—early. I found him around ten o'-clock in the morning."

"And Rachael died about then, too. I don't know anything about the Meyer baby, do you?"

"No. But when I went to the store that day it was early, before nine. Should I just put down a question mark for his time of death?"

"Yes. I don't know how we'll find out, though."

"Let's not worry about the hows right now," Janaan said quickly. "Let's just keep going. We've come up with a lot already. Think!"

Lauren pulled her knees to her chin and wrapped her arms around her legs. A cool breeze made her shiver. She tried to visualize the babies, tried to sense them in her mind's eye. "I know something!" she shouted. "Adam was Moslem and Rachael was Jewish."

"Pardon me, but those are hardly the same," Janaan broke in.

"I know, except they're both Middle Eastern religions. We need to think in broader terms. Do you know what religion the Meyers are?"

"No."

"Okay, we need to find out. What if they're Jewish? Or Moslem? Maybe it was a religious thing."

Janaan narrowed her eyes. "You know, it is kind of odd that the babies have Middle Eastern ties. When I went to the mosque with my dad, I noticed that there just aren't that many Moslems in these parts. And we don't seem to have a huge Jewish population, either. Doesn't that seem strange to you?"

Nodding excitedly, Lauren exclaimed, "You bet it does. And something else could be important."

"What?"

"The feelings between the Moslems and the Jews.

What if it were some sort of political thing? All you have to do is turn on the news to see the problems in Israel. Look at how upset your father was when you came sitting with me at the Blooms.

"Laurie?"

"Wait a minute! What's your dad's license plate number? The day Rachael died, I saw a blue car just like his driving by the Blooms' house. . . . " Lauren's voice trailed off.

"What are you trying to say!" Janaan demanded, her eyes blazing.

"People do all kinds of things in the name of religion," Lauren faltered.

Janaan reached over to grip Lauren's arm tightly. "If you're thinking my dad could have anything to do with this, don't say it." She held up her hand as Lauren began to protest. "I mean it. Don't even say it. First of all, my dad and mom were together the whole day when Rachael died. They're in this real intense counseling that lasts hours. And secondly, and I really mean this, I don't know how I would feel about you if you accused my father of murder."

"I didn't!" Lauren pulled her arm free. "Why are you suddenly so defensive? You're the one who told me how impossible he's been to live with and how superpolitical he's become."

"I also said we'd made some real progress. Look, Laurie, you're my best friend, but there are some lines even you can't cross. My father would never have hurt a child, his or anyone else's. Case closed."

"Fine."

They sat in silence on the grass. Lauren opened her mouth to speak, but closed it again. Neither of them said a word. After what seemed like ages Lauren looked from under lowered eyelids at Janaan.

"You mad?"

"No."

"Do you want to leave?"

"Not yet. I want to keep working on this. And . . ."

"And?"

"And, my father's license plate is APAG-1."

Lauren shook her head. "That's not the one I saw. And I'm sorry I upset you so much."

"It's okay. Let's just drop it." Janaan picked up the pen she'd thrown to the grass. "The religious angle really is a good one. I mean, Jews and Moslems are minorities in these parts, so it's against the odds for Kevin Meyer to be one or the other. Let's assume he was Jewish. Besides a crazed madman on a vendetta, what could be important about it?"

"Politics?"

"Besides that. There's got to be something else."

"Well, the traditions seem awfully similar to me," Lauren began. "In a lot of ways your family and Rachael's family do things the same. . . ."

Lauren froze. All the pieces, all the bits of information fell together to make a chilling picture.

"What things? Would you please finish your sentences! The way you do that drives me crazy!"

"I'm thinking!" Gooseflesh crept up Lauren's arms. The idea was too incredible, too bizarre. But if the third baby was Moslem, or even Jewish, it could be possible.

"What? You look like you've seen a ghost. What is it?"

"Suppose . . ." Lauren looked at Janaan's expectant face. She bit her lip, then turned away. It wouldn't be fair to tell Janaan, not yet. Not until she was sure.

"Look, we're supposed to be in this together," Janaan said, annoyed. "If you've thought of something, tell me!"

"I—it's probably nothing, really. If the Meyer baby fits the pattern, well, then I promise I'll tell."

She grabbed the paper and jumped to her feet. "I want to go over this sheet tonight, okay? Meet me after school tomorrow, and be sure you wear a dress."

"A dress?"

"A conservative dress. We're going to play detective."

13

Word about Janaan had circulated around Skyline. Lauren tried to stay with her as much as possible. Snatches of gossip followed them as they passed, hanging in the air like smoke in a closed room.

"Not enough evidence . . ."

"Did you hear . . . ?"

"Three gone . . ."

"Murder . . ."

"Let's hit the cafeteria before they take the skin off the pudding," Lauren suggested, to distract her. "We need to go over our next move."

"Are you going to tell me?"

"Tell you what?"

"About your idea. The one that hit you at Sugar Lake yesterday. Come on, Laurie, you're driving me crazy!"

Lauren pulled her binder close to her chest. Sleep had eluded her most of the night as she tossed and turned, consumed by the eerie connection that played through her mind. It was tempting to share her idea with Janaan, but she knew she couldn't. Not until she had one more piece of the puzzle. And even if she were right, how could she ever find the words to tell her? Janaan was so tense it seemed she would snap any minute. No, Lauren decided, it's definitely better to wait until I find out what religion Mrs. Meyer is. And if her plan worked, the answer would be just a few hours away.

"I was up most of the night thinking, and I've come up with a way to get the information on Mrs. Meyer," Lauren replied, deliberately evading Janaan's question. "I'll tell it to you over lunch. Of course, I'm using the term *lunch* loosely. Today's special looks like leftovers from biology lab."

She tried to keep her voice bright, but Janaan wasn't listening. As the two of them walked by, clusters of girls broke apart, their eyes riveting on Janaan's every movement.

It was a strange sort of isolation. Lauren and Janaan had always been a part of this group, as indistinguishable as one grain of sand from another. They'd lived in a comfortable middle ground, neither superstars nor outcasts; as part of a whole, they'd thought of themselves as students in a student body. Now they were different, Lauren realized. Stigma covered them like a glass bell, separating them with invisible but very real walls.

"I don't feel like eating, especially around these snakes. This is what I meant when I said they'd wonder about me." Janaan's eyes flared. "I can't stand being the center of gossip. It was a mistake to come back."

"Except we need to graduate. We've still got two more weeks. . . ."

"You've got two more weeks. I'm through until things get straightened out. And as if I didn't have enough problems, here comes Cynthia."

Bouncing up the hallway in a lavender tank top and faded denim skirt came Cynthia Walker, her eyelashes mascaraed into what Lauren called eye-fangs, her bleached hair held with so much mousse it looked lacquered.

"Hey, Lauren, Janaan, I haven't seen you guys for a couple of days," Cynthia said, talking in exclamation points. "I've heard a lot, though, and I must say, I'm impressed! My scandals aren't half as interesting!" As she leaned closer, Lauren was overwhelmed with Cynthia's lily-of-the-valley cologne.

"I just want you to know, Janaan," Cynthia went on, "even though we haven't always gotten along, I'm positive you didn't do it. The whole stupid thing stinks. I know you've got Lauren, but if you need anything, anything at all, you can count on me."

There was a silence. Janaan's eyes widened until they seemed almost round.

"Thanks, Cynthia," she finally said. "You're the only one besides Laurie . . ."

"No thanks necessary. If people are going to talk, it might as well be about something you've actually done. Anyway, I've got to run to the little-girls' room. See you around!" She glanced back at Janaan, gave a half smile, and added, "By the way, did you do something to your hair?"

"No," Janaan answered.

"You should think about it." She laughed as she stepped around them and hurried away.

"Well," Lauren whispered, "I never thought I'd see the day. Of all our supposed friends, she's the only one to show an ounce of support. And she's not even what we've ever called a friend."

Janaan watched silently as Cynthia disappeared into the lavatory. Finally, she turned to Lauren and said softly, "She must go through this kind of stuff all the time. She comes to school every day, and hardly anyone likes her. If she can . . ." Janaan squared her shoulders. "Let's go eat."

Lauren handed a clipboard to Janaan and asked nervously, "You ready?"

"As ready as I'll ever be. I hate people who do this."

"I'm listening if you've got a better idea."

They slid out of the car and began walking up Sterling Avenue. The older homes had a comfortable look to them, a sort of well-worn coziness that reminded Lauren of gingerbread houses. White and bisque-colored curtains ruffled the windows, wooden shingles layered the pitched roofs. Further down, a lawn sprinkler gently spun water ribbons into the air.

"One-oh-eight—that's her house," Lauren whispered.

"Then let's start next door."

The house in front of them looked darker than the others, its leaded glass dulled by a layer of dust. Keeping an eye on Mrs. Meyer's house, they rang the bell of the next-door neighbor and waited. Even though it was eighty-nine degrees in the shade, Lauren's hands felt cold. The door cracked open and an eye, pale and bloodshot, looked them over.

"You sellin' somethin'—'cause if ya are I'm not interested."

Lauren cleared her throat. "We're not selling anything. We're here to do a survey."

"Oh, yeah? What kind?"

The door opened wider, and a man glared at them. Gray stubble bristled across his lined face, and his hair, thin and oily-white, was combed straight back. His stomach hung over like a sack of flour, cinched up by a belt that dug into disproportionately small hips.

"Well, you wanna know what kinda soap I use or what?" he growled.

"We're doing a social studies report on the demographics of religion in America. We're correlating race and different beliefs, charting them, and then determining how likely it would be for a person of a certain ethnic group to be a member of a certain religion," Lauren chattered. She prayed she sounded official.

"You want to know what religion I am? Let me tell you something—when I got up this morning, this was still America. And in America, my religion is none of your damn business!" The door slammed so hard it made them both jump.

"Way to go," Janaan said dryly. "I'm in on this and even I didn't understand what you said. Let's try the other side. And keep an eye out for Mrs. Meyer!"

The house on the south side of the Meyers' was brown brick. Although it was only six in the evening and still as bright as noontime, the porch light had been turned on and every window shone with soft yellow light. They decided Janaan should do the survey this time. She rang the bell, then rang again. Finally a chain slid and a middle-aged woman stood at the door.

"Yes?"

"We're doing a survey for our social studies class, and we wondered if we could ask you a few questions. It shouldn't take long, and we'd really appreciate your help," Janaan said, smiling brilliantly. "Our grade is at stake."

"I'm cooking, but I have a few minutes, if that's enough. You two really shouldn't do this at the dinner hour."

"I'm sorry. I'll try to make it fast. What we're doing is writing down the race of the people, then their religion, and trying to make a correlation between the two. For example, you'd call yourself white, wouldn't you?"

"Caucasian."

"Right, Caucasian. And would you consider yourself a Protestant?"

"No, I'm Catholic. Is there anything else?" she asked, glancing over her shoulder.

"Yes," Lauren broke in. "We've been to the house next door two different times, but we never seem to catch them home. We really need to get this done—could you help?"

"Well," the woman said, rubbing her forehead, "I know they're white. As for their religion, it's some weird kind of thing, one I've never heard of."

"Is it Moslem?" Janaan asked.

"No . . ."

"Jewish?" Lauren said, excitement edging her voice.

"Heavens, no, I've heard of them. Let me think, what do they call it? Oh, yes. Baha'i. That's it. Baha'i. Now if you two don't mind, I really must get back to my stove. Good luck on your report!"

Baha'i. It didn't fit. Disappointment welled inside Lauren. She'd almost talked herself into the idea, had somewhere along the way convinced herself she was right.

"So, does that answer the burning question? Are you going to come clean and explain this great theory of yours?" Janaan asked.

Turning to go, Lauren snapped, "There's no point. I was wrong. I'd like to drop it, okay?"

"You could at least tell me. . . ."

Janaan didn't get any further. The doorway to the Meyer home flew open and Cathy Meyer stormed out. Her pale face was a mixture of terror and fury, and even though she'd seemed a small woman at Lauren's home, she now swelled with rage.

"It's Lauren Taylor, isn't it? And Janaan! I've been watching you through my window—how dare you come here?"

Her voice was loud and shrill. Lauren looked around quickly, then began walking toward her. Janaan hung back.

"You come any closer and I'm calling the police! I want to know what you're doing here!"

"Wait a minute!" Lauren pleaded. "Just hear me out."

"Why should I? You're a friend of that girl . . ."

"Let me get close enough so I don't have to shout. Please."

Lauren saw a flicker of indecision. She took three more steps forward.

"What do you want!"

"Janaan didn't do anything—you've got to believe that."

"My baby's body is missing! I don't know what happened to him, but she"—Cathy jerked her head at Janaan—"had something to do with it! What are you two, witches? Are you members of some horrid coven that . . ."

"We're not witches," Lauren told her quickly. "All I need to know is two things. First, what time did Kevin die?"

Cathy Meyer flushed with anger. "You think for one minute I'd tell you anything?"

"I know you're upset, but . . ."

"I'm calling the police!"

"No!"

"She's a murderer!"

"Janaan's innocent. . . ."

"You believe that? You could be a killer, too!"

"*Stop it!*"

Lauren whirled to see Janaan standing behind her, her fists clenched so tightly the veins stood out. She looked from Lauren to Cathy. "I am living through hell because I held your baby."

Her voice, her entire body trembled, and her eyes blurred with tears. "That's all I did. I held a little baby because I thought he looked like Adam."

"Janny . . ." Lauren began.

"I don't even know why I'm here." Janaan brushed a tear from her cheek. "I don't know why this is happening to me. I just thought he looked like Adam." A sob raked through her, full of despair.

Lauren put her arm around Janaan and began to lead her away.

"Little Kevin died at nine-thirty in the morning."

"What?" Lauren asked, startled.

"I said," Cathy Meyer repeated coldly, "he died at nine-thirty in the morning. Is there something else you wanted to know? If there is, you've got one minute."

Something about Janaan must have touched her, made her doubt just enough to help. Lauren quickly pressed her advantage.

"I just need to know one more thing. How long after he died did you bury him? Please!" Lauren's voice was desperate.

"He was buried that same night. It's part of our faith."

"Then he wasn't embalmed?"

"No." Cathy Meyer yanked open her door then turned back to face them. "When I saw Janaan at your house, I knew. My husband begged me not to call the police, but I remembered her from that day. And now, the two of you are standing here, at my home, and I don't know what to think any more." She clutched the doorknob. "But let me tell you this—if you really did kill my baby, I'll pray until I take my last breath that God will repay you a thousandfold. I'll pray both of you die!"

Without another word, she disappeared into the darkened entryway of her house. The door closed firmly behind her.

14

"I have to go home."

The flatness in Janaan's voice dismayed Lauren. Somehow, in the late wash of sun, Janaan had faded. Her honey skin had paled to ashen, her green eyes had cooled to steel.

But Lauren herself felt as though she were going to burst, to shoot colors out of every pore. Because she knew. The piece fit.

"Did you hear what she said?" Lauren began excitedly. "The babies . . ."

"I heard enough. I want to go."

"But, Janny . . ."

Janaan started to half walk, half run, toward the parked car. Her high heels scraped along the walkway.

"Wait for me, I have something to tell you," Lauren cried, running after her.

"This is a waste of time. Why do I set myself up? That woman hates me!" Janaan flung the clipboard into a clump of hedges. "They all do!"

"Quit running away!" Lauren caught Janaan's elbow

and spun her around. "Janny, listen to me! I was right! Adam died on a Thursday morning. He was buried that night, right?"

"Let go of me. I don't want to hear any more!"

Lauren tightened her grip. "And Rachael, she died on a Wednesday. And she was buried that night. And now Kevin Meyer. He was buried the same day he died. Don't you see it?"

"What? What am I supposed to see? Three babies die, three babies are buried. What do you want from me?"

They stood beside the car now. Lauren dropped her hand from Janaan's arm, but their eyes remained locked. Adrenaline raced through her. Even her blood seemed to throb. She drew in a sharp breath. "Maybe they aren't dead. Any of them. Janny, I think your brother could be alive!"

The grayness that had overtaken Janaan departed, instantly replaced by fire. Her green eyes blazed.

"You're sick!"

"No! Hear me out!"

"You're sick! Leave me alone!" Janaan ran to the driver's side of her car and yanked on the handle. It was locked. She pawed through her purse in a frantic search for her keys.

Lauren stood stunned. Janaan had refused to even hear her. She raced around the car, but Janaan wouldn't face her.

"Why were those three chosen?" Lauren demanded.

"I don't know!"

"Why those religions?"

"I don't know!"

"Why were they all buried the same day they died?"

"It doesn't matter!" Janaan dumped the entire contents of her purse onto the street.

"Yes, it does! Just listen a minute! Adam could be alive! I feel it!"

"You won't stop, will you?" Janaan spat. "Do you know how hard this has been on me? Do you? I was there. I found him in his crib. I tried to give him mouth-to-mouth resuscitation, but he was already cold." She grabbed her keys, glinting gold in the pile of plastic combs and brushes. "Do you honestly think you can find something every single policeman, every single detective, missed? And what about the doctor that examined Adam? Was that man so stupid that he couldn't tell a dead baby from a live one? Or didn't you think of that!" She began to stuff the mess back into her purse.

Lauren crouched down beside her, her full cotton skirt flaring against the asphalt. "I'm just asking you to consider the possibility."

Janaan ignored her.

Lauren didn't know what to do. She'd been afraid it might be too much to tell Janaan, and yet, when Cathy Meyer confirmed that the third baby had been buried within hours of its death, her theory connected into a perfect pattern. It was like a tapestry, viewed first from the back with all its loops and knots snarled together, suddenly flipped over to reveal a clear picture. She had to force Janaan to look at the picture, even if she didn't want to.

"There were things I kept wondering about, things that didn't make sense," Lauren began. Janaan grabbed at scraps of papers fluttering away in a breeze. "Like who would want the body of a child? Why would anyone risk going to prison for a corpse? I couldn't see a reason. Then, when we were sitting at Sugar Lake, I thought about Adam's funeral—how quickly Moslems bury their dead. Then I thought of Rachael and how they buried her the same way. Rachael and Adam weren't embalmed. Neither was Kevin Meyer, we just found out. And suddenly it came to me. Maybe they were chosen for that very reason."

"No!" Janaan sprang to her feet. "It's like Cathy Meyer said, a coven or an insane person took their bodies." Her hands shook as she tried to push the key into the lock. "I've buried my brother once. Don't make me do it again."

She unlocked the door, but Lauren blocked her way, suddenly realizing how close Janaan was to going under. She'd been treading emotional water since Adam died, barely keeping her head above the crashing waves. Adam's death, her parents' problems, Rachael's death, the investigation—all had run together to form an undertow that was dragging her down. Now Lauren had thrown one more wave over her, and Janaan looked as though she might drown.

Lauren's voice dropped to murmur, "Don't go."

Janaan pulled on the door, but Lauren leaned against it. "I don't blame you if you won't stop for me, but for God's sake, stop for Adam."

Janaan froze. A bird chirped from a nearby tree, its sweet song suddenly shrill in the silence. For an instant neither one of them moved, as though they were a photograph captured on a living backdrop. Finally the moment broke. Turning to face her, Janaan stared at Lauren with a shadow of wild hope in her eyes.

Lauren felt her heart beat again. "I know it sounds impossible, but I think Adam's alive," she whispered. "They all are. And if you help me, I know somehow we can find them!"

Lauren nestled into her porch swing and stared at the night. It was one of those velvety skies, where the stars hang like brilliant stones against the darkness. She curled one foot underneath her and pushed slowly, rhythmically, comforted by the familiar creak of the wood. Out on their hill, insects sang.

Watching as the moon scuttled from behind a single cloud, Lauren's eyes drifted to the pools of liquid shadow cast beneath the trees. Familiar things hid in that inky blackness, impossible to see even though she knew they were there. A ring of star-of-Bethlehem, a patch of violets, a mound of rocks to mark where she'd buried a bird years ago—all were there, but imperceptible in the darkness. Like the answers she needed. She could feel their presence, but the solutions remained as hidden as those flowers.

She might never be able to find the babies, and if she couldn't, then what? Janaan wouldn't ever let it go, not now. Lauren pushed the swing harder and lifted the hair off her neck. She was responsible for the hope ignited in Janaan. Just hours before, she'd been so sure of herself, so hell-bent to convince Janaan she was right that nothing else seemed to matter. She'd won—Janaan believed her now. But what if she were wrong? What if the babies really were dead? She'd be responsible for raising a false hope Janaan would cling to forever.

"Laurie?" Her mother's voice called through the screen door, "Janny's here. Do you want her to come out there with you?"

"What time is it?"

"Almost ten. She says it's important."

"Sure, send her back." Pricks of apprehension needled Lauren's back.

The door banged shut as Janaan stepped onto the porch. She was dressed in black acid-washed jeans and a long-sleeved navy cotton shirt. A belt of some dark color cinched her waist—even her shoes were black leather high-tops. It was an odd outfit for such a hot night.

"It's dark out here. I need some light, do you mind?" Janaan asked, flipping on the porch light.

"Turn it off, Janny," Lauren said, squinting. "The moths will head straight for the light and I hate breathing bugs."

"That's okay, we won't be here long." She came closer until she stood beside Lauren. "I had a fight with my dad about leaving so late, but it was only a five on the parental Richter scale. He really is trying. You want to know something?"

"What?"

"He told me the government shut down the Arab information office in Washington."

"Oh. That's too bad," Lauren said flatly.

"It really is. He was in a horrible mood, but this is the first time I can remember him telling me why. He actually talked to me as if I had the capacity to understand—which I did. There still is a lot of discrimination. . . ."

"Is that what you came over for, to talk politics?" Lauren broke in impatiently.

"Excuse me. I thought you might be interested in knowing I had an actual conversation with my father without coming to blows, but I can see you're a wee bit testy tonight. What's wrong?"

Lauren sighed. "Nothing."

"Hey, you should be feeling great right now. I am. All through dinner I kept thinking of seeing Adam again." She looked around quickly, then lowered her voice. "You haven't told anyone. . . ."

"No. Of course not!"

"Good." Janaan flashed a smile. "I think you were right when you said our parents would go to the police with it, and they'll just somehow turn it against me. There's no way I'm giving those Neanderthals more rope to hang me with."

Leaning against the brick wall to watch Lauren, Janaan asked her, "Have you thought of what we should do next?"

"No. Anyway, it's late. I'm tired. My mom said you

had something important to tell me. You've got the floor." Lauren couldn't seem to keep the shortness from her voice.

Janaan's smile was suddenly gone. "What is with you?"

"I *said*, nothing!"

"Bull!"

Without meeting Janaan's eyes, Lauren ran her hand up and down the swing's dull metal chain, seeming to count each oval link. Janaan stared silently, waiting. Finally she broke the silence. "You're scared you're wrong, aren't you?"

Lauren's voice was tight. "I don't know, maybe. It's not just that, it's . . ."

"You're afraid we'll never find them and I'll have a nervous breakdown and end up in a sanatorium. Then you'll think it's all your fault and be overcome with guilt for the rest of your life. Am I right?"

"Am I that obvious?"

"No, I just know you that well. Listen, Laurie, I realize we could be wrong. I also realize finding them's a long shot, and I know how much harder it's going to be without the police. But something inside tells me we're going to make it. The thing is, it won't work if either one of us looks back."

Janaan sat next to Lauren. She began to push the swing gently.

"You remember when we went out for pizza at Fred's? And the way I sort of jumped all over you?"

Lauren nodded. "I remember."

There was a pause. Janaan drew in a breath and continued. "I'm sorry for the things I said to you. You were right, you know. I was jealous."

"But, Janaan, that's so crazy," Lauren protested. "I've always envied you. You're a lot prettier than I am, and thin and athletic. . . ."

"I'm short and scrawny. Don't be an idiot, Laurie. Everybody loves a tall blond. But that's not the part that got to me. Your whole family is so normal—I mean, you're the only person I know who really likes her parents. It's obviously mutual. I just wanted so much to have a family like yours and to be like you. I wanted to be you."

The swing stopped. Lauren turned to look at Janaan. She didn't know what to say.

"The thing is, Laurie, I might get my brother back. I understand my dad for the first time in forever, and, well, it doesn't seem so bad to be me anymore. I owe you that. You've stuck it out even when I pushed you away. And I want you to know I'm grateful." She looked out into the night.

"I—I wasn't all that wonderful," Lauren answered, embarrassed. "After the pizza, I sort of vowed never to speak to you again." She didn't want to admit her disloyalty, yet she couldn't take credit for being something she wasn't. "I shouldn't have jumped on you when you told me about your dad. I didn't really give you a chance to tell your side."

"You gave me plenty of chances," Janaan declared firmly. "You always have. I just didn't take them."

They began to swing again. The night air caught strands of Lauren's hair, twisting them into gold chains across her face. She pulled them away and began to braid her hair.

"You know," she said thoughtfully, "I'm sorry about that night, too. I said some pretty awful things about your father, and now I wish I hadn't."

"It's funny how that works, isn't it?" Janaan laughed. "I could call him a bastard in one breath and in the next breath kill anyone who put him down."

Lauren murmured, "I think that means you love him."

"I do. But we'll have to talk about that another night." She slapped her hands on her knees, then jumped to her feet.

"Where are you going?" Lauren asked.

"Not where am *I* going, but where are *we* going!" she said, grabbing Lauren's arm and pulling her to her feet. "You have to change your outfit."

"But I don't want to go anywhere," Lauren argued.

"Sorry, you can't back out now."

"Out of what? What are you talking about?"

"A way to find my brother. That's why I'm here. You might not have a plan, but I do!"

15

"Where are we going?" Lauren asked.

Janaan rifled Lauren's closet, pulled out a forest green turtleneck and a pair of jeans and tossed them on the bed. "Do you have a black stocking cap?" she asked.

"Sure," Lauren answered, "I always keep one handy in case there's a summer snow."

"Seriously, you need one. Your hair is so light it's practically neon." Janaan took a box with winter scarves and hats from Lauren's closet shelf and rummaged through them until she found a navy knit cap.

"That won't even fit my head. That's my ski-camp hat from sixth grade! Look, I cross-stitched my name on the front."

"It'll stretch. Besides, I think the name is kinda cute. Put it in your purse till we get outside."

Lauren ran her hand through her hair and watched as Janaan searched her dresser. "Aha!" Janaan exclaimed, pulling out black knee-highs. "These, too!"

"I'm not putting anything on until you tell me what

we're doing. One thing's for sure, I'm not breaking in to some building."

"Of course not!" Janaan's voice was hushed. "Keep it down, your folks'll hear. It's no big secret, I just wanted to wait until we were in your room. I had to be sure we'd have absolute privacy." She held up a pair of black sneakers from the bottom of the closet with a triumphant smile.

"Perfect. We need dark colors, but I don't want your parents to suspect anything. It'll have to look like an outfit."

Eyeing the clothes Janaan had picked out, Lauren asked, "Are we going to an extremely casual funeral?"

Janaan jumped beside her on the bed. "No, but you're close. We're going to the cemetery."

A cemetery at night—the thought made Lauren's heart shiver. Graveyards were fine during the day, but the dark transformed them into the haunted gatherings of her nightmares. At thirteen, she and a friend had gone to the graveyard Halloween night. Maybe it was her own breath frosting in the cold air, but to Lauren it had seemed as though generations of spirits drifted vaporlike through the tombstones, brushing against her cheeks and fingering her hair. Footsteps scraped behind them, crunching the dead leaves. They'd screamed and run back so fast the air knifed their lungs. Four years later she still shuddered, picturing that night and the fear that had gripped her.

"Oh, no!" Lauren said, shaking her head, "I'll go

with you tomorrow, but I'm not running around a cemetery in the dark!"

"We have to!" Janaan said.

"No, we don't! There's not a person in there that's leaving!"

Softly, Janaan answered, "Three babies did."

Lauren chewed her fingernail.

Her voice brisk again, Janaan went on, "Come on, Laurie, don't be such a baby. Now listen, I found something out. I went to the library and looked up Kevin Meyer's obituary, and guess what? He was buried at Mountain Rest Cemetery. That's the same cemetery Adam and Rachael were buried in."

"There isn't another graveyard around here, so I think that was fairly obvious, Janny."

"You're forgetting Mount Holy Oak, the Catholic Cemetery."

"I know, but we already figured out the religious angle. Catholics embalm."

"That's just it. We still haven't figured how he got them out. Now whoever did this had to have access to the cemetery, but couldn't risk taking the babies when they could be seen. He or she would have to work at night."

"So?" Lauren asked.

"So if you think about it, the only logical thing to do is go to the place the crime was committed at the time it would have been committed. We're going to have to be our own detectives, Laurie. We'll have to think like they would."

"Listen to yourself! The only people you've seen re-create a crime were on television! This isn't the movies, Janny, and we don't have a script to follow. This is real! We could get in serious trouble if we're caught!"

"But it could work!" Janaan bounced the mattress in excitement. "Look, we can creep around for a little while and see if we find something unusual, like some-one driving to the cemetery in the middle of the night, or walking around like they're checking things out. Or maybe even digging up a grave! Whoever took Adam has been there before, and could come again. I'll just bet he'd come out at night."

Janaan was talking fast, her words piling one on top of the other to wall Lauren in.

"I don't want to do this! Let's just go in the morning, okay?" Lauren pleaded.

"The police have been all over that place in the day-light, and they haven't found a thing! Besides, dressed like this, no one will see us. We'll practically be ghosts ourselves!"

"I know you want me to do this," Lauren said, shak-ing her head slowly. "But honestly, Janaan, I don't see the point. It's such a long shot. . . ."

"Then I'll do it myself."

"No! We'll just think of another way!"

Folding her arms across her chest, Janaan snapped, "Okay. I'm listening. You tell me how we're going to find Adam and Rachael. What's your plan? I believe you, Laurie. I think they're alive. Now what?"

With the palms of her hands, Lauren rubbed her eyes.

She knew Janaan was watching her expectantly, but what could she say? She'd gone over it in her mind a thousand times. Who took them? How did they do it? Why couldn't the doctors tell they were alive? And where could she start finding answers? Janaan's plan was thin, but what better choice could Lauren offer? Finally she dropped her hands to her lap.

"We'd only stay a little while?"

"Guaranteed." Janaan flashed a victorious smile. "We'll just snoop around and see what we can see, then leave. I swear. And I'll hold your hand the whole time."

Between the twisting wrought-iron bars Lauren saw the tombstones, gleaming as though freshly white-washed by the moon. The headstones crowded together behind the gate, like row upon row of granite ghosts. Lauren shivered. Janaan had followed her into the living room when she'd told her parents they were leaving for a Coke, and she'd silently prayed they would question her, notice her clothes or the strained look on her face. Neither one of them looked up.

"Be back soon, honey," was the only thing her father had mumbled as he hunched at his desk, slowly pecking his typewriter. Her mother had been so engrossed in a novel she'd barely grunted good-bye. So Lauren had found herself here, outside a closed cemetery at ten-forty at night.

"It's locked. Can we go now?"

"I already told you they'd be closed. That's the whole idea—whoever'd be here now shouldn't be." She pulled

Lauren's stocking cap from her back pocket. "Tried to leave it behind, didn't you? Put it on, and be sure to tuck all your hair up."

"Can't we just look through the bars?" Lauren begged.

"What good will that do? See that tree down there against the fence? It's perfect for climbing! We'll just grab that lower limb and pull ourselves over." Janaan tugged on her arm. "Come on!"

The graveyard was far enough out of town that the street seemed lifeless. One car passed them, its headlights piercing the darkness like lasers, and then it was gone. The limb of the tree stretched over the five-foot fence and drooped slightly toward the sidewalk. It was still a reach for Janaan, so Lauren stood behind and helped push her up and over. Leaves trembled and shook as Lauren pulled on the branch, holding it like a rope as she walked up the grate. She grabbed another higher limb, balanced herself, then jumped over to the ground. Her breath came in sharp pants as she looked for Janaan. It was deathly quiet. Lauren's chest squeezed as she whispered, "Janny! Where are you?"

"Right here!"

"God!" Lauren exploded, twirling around. "Don't do that! I almost had a heart attack. . . ."

"Sorry."

Lauren crouched down next to Janaan. Blades of grass tickled her skin.

"What now? I can hardly see a thing!" she whispered.

"Let's walk along the edge of the road. I'm not scared

of cemeteries the way you are, but I hate stepping on graves. I thought we could pretty much follow the road to the top of the hill. That way we can see in every direction."

They stayed near the shoulder, ready to dive between tombstones if a car drove by, but none did. Warm night air rustled treetops. The grass smelled fresh. A few springtime locusts buzzed. The sounds and smells were familiar here, like an evening in her own backyard. There were no telephone wires to slice up the night sky, just a galaxy of stars hanging low enough to touch. Lauren felt herself relax. This place didn't seem fearful. It felt peaceful. She thought of herself four years earlier, a skinny thirteen-year-old paralyzed with terror at the thought of spirits.

Her imagination had fanned a spark of fear into an inferno, and now, as she looked around her, she realized nothing frightening was there. It reminded her of a time she and her dad had visited the house she'd been born in, when all the gigantic rooms, towering ceilings, and winding stairs had no longer loomed large, as in her memories, but had become strangely dwarfed. Her father had chuckled and said, "It just looks different because your perspective's different. Things always change if you see them from a higher place."

"Look over there," Janaan whispered, breaking into her thoughts, pointing toward some trees. "There's a guy wearing a hockey mask. Maybe he wants to play with us!"

"Nice try, Janny. I've already decided I'm not scared

anymore. Now get serious. You're supposed to be searching for clues."

They walked on in silence. There was a time when Janaan's joking would have fooled Lauren, but now she seemed to see her friend, too, from a higher place. Janaan had guarded her emotions like a pit bull, but they were there, all of them. Jealousy, love, tenacity, fear, all brewing under layers of bright chatter.

In the process of seeing inside Janaan, Lauren had discovered something about herself, too. She'd been able to exist under pressure. Detectives had challenged her and she hadn't caved in—she'd been stretched and come out okay. Lauren smiled to herself. She was tougher than she thought.

"What's that up ahead?"

"Janny . . . !"

"I'm not kidding this time! Someone's coming! Get down!"

She pulled Lauren behind a gravestone just as a caretaker's truck rumbled by. Its white paint gleamed silver in the moonlight, and its truckbed held tools that stood like quills on an animal. The truck slowed, then turned left up a narrow drive. Soon the taillight disappeared behind a hill.

"There's something!" Janaan whispered. "It's a little late to be mowing the grass, don't you think? Let's see where it's going!"

They followed the drive an eighth of a mile until they reached its crest. From there they saw a distant string of streetlights marking the cemetery's eastern edge. At the bottom of the hill an old brick house overlooked a sea of graves. Its tall beveled windows, webbed with black lines from jutting tree limbs, glowed yellow in the night. The white truck stood parked at the edge of the driveway.

"What should we do now?" Lauren whispered.

A shadowy figure moved against the lighted windows.

"Somebody's walking around inside. Let's get closer and see who it is."

"It's just the groundskeeper," Lauren answered.

"Maybe."

"What if we get caught?"

"Tell him your cat jumped the fence and ask if he's seen it."

"Janny," Lauren said, catching her arm, "why are we doing this? I don't like to spy on people."

It was hard to see Janaan in the dark, but Lauren could feel her muscles tighten.

"Have you ever seen that truck before?" she asked in a low voice.

"I don't know—there're a lot of white trucks on the road. Why?"

"I can't explain it, but it's like déjà vu. Something about it clicked with me. I—I just can't place why or where. . . ."

Lauren took a step backward. "I think you're talking yourself into this. Look, Janny, I'm not going to hold it over you if we don't find anything."

"You're not listening to me! I'm serious! I think we

should get a look at this man." Their hushed voices rose.

"What if he sees us?" Lauren protested. "You're in enough trouble with the police as it is."

"He won't! We'll get inside the hedge and peek through the very bottom of the window."

"This is ridiculous!"

The whites of Janaan's eyes and her teeth glinted in the moonlight. "This could be important, and all you're worried about is covering your behind. Wait here then! I'll do it myself." Crouching low, Janaan took a step toward the house.

"I hate it when you do that! Quit trying to pressure me!" Lauren called after her.

Janaan turned back. "We pressure each other. That's how we've made it this far." She began to creep down the hill.

Lauren looked from Janaan's dark figure to the glowing windows of the house. Janaan was right. They were a balance, like yin and yang. Maybe that was the reason their friendship survived, because by pulling at each other they made themselves stronger.

She took a deep breath. "Wait! I'm coming with you!"

"Keep your head down," Janaan warned. "And for heaven's sake keep quiet!"

They crept slowly, cautiously, like two cats eyeing a bird. A gnarled five-foot-high thicket surrounded the house, its cropped branches barely skimming the front window ledge. The movement was coming from behind that window. A pair of heavy gold drapes had been drawn open, but the view was shrouded by panels of sheer curtains.

Lauren pulled at the thicket, trying to make a space large enough for the two of them to crawl through. Twigs snapped and popped, tiny spines of wood scraped their skin, but they finally pushed inside the hedge. Janaan dug her feet into the base of the thick roots and cautiously reached her fingers to the sill. Lauren was tall enough to peer inside.

The man had left the living room. They could hear the rattle of dishes in the background and could see a shadow on a patch of hallway.

"There must be a kitchen back there," Lauren whispered.

"Shhh. Just look."

The room had been decorated in a strange style. Although the house itself looked to be more than a hundred years old, its tiny vaulted-ceiling living room, which seemed created for brocade and silver tea carts, was now filled with a chaotic blend of rough wooden art and breezy rattan. Even through the sheers Lauren could tell it was dirty. A film of dust had settled on painted masks that hung across the walls, and a layer of grime dimmed the sofa's palm-leaf pattern. Two wicker end tables held an assortment of oddities: dried weeds, shells, a hollowed horn, a piece of bone. Lauren's eyes roamed the room. More strange junk crammed the shelves of a bookcase. A pile of clothes lay scattered in the hallway.

"This place should be condemned!" Lauren said under her breath, as Janaan strained to see inside. The sharp end of a branch bored into Lauren's back, and her sweater stuck against the rough brick.

"He's not coming back to the living room," she hissed to Janaan. "We can't stand here forever—this hedge is killing me!"

"Oh, my God!" Janaan grabbed Lauren's arm so tightly she almost cried out in pain. With a shaking finger, Janaan pointed to the clothing that lay on the floor.

"What is it?"

"Look there, in the corner."

Lauren's eyes searched the crumpled shirts and underwear. Then she saw it. A piece of child's clothing lay tossed against the others. It was a small sailor suit, navy with red piping.

Janaan's voice shook. "That's the outfit my brother was buried in!"

Suddenly a shadow loomed over the clothing. A thin, dark, hollow-chested man slid into the room, sucking a cigarette and holding a leather book.

Lauren looked wildly from the man to the truck parked behind her, then back at the man. Flicking ashes off the end of his cigarette, he grabbed the empty horn from the end table, then crossed back to the hallway and disappeared.

Lauren's heart pounded so hard the vein throbbed in her throat. Finally she managed to whisper hoarsely, "That's the same man that helped me get Rachael from

Marjorie! He was there the day she died! We've got to get out of here!"

As they backed out, the hedge seemed to grab them. Its branches became groping arms, the twigs turning into grasping fingers that hooked into their clothing and hair. When she tried to pull herself free, Lauren's knit cap caught in the thicket. Her long blond hair spilled into the thorns and held her.

"Janny, help me!"

Janaan's hands shook as she pulled strands of Lauren's hair from the hedge. Seconds went by, but to Lauren time hung suspended, an eternity. One piece of hair, then another. Lauren could feel her head loosening.

"I'm almost done."

A hand clamped down hard on Lauren's shoulder. She heard Janaan gasp.

"Make a sound," a harsh voice warned, "and I'll cut this one's neck in two."

16

The six-inch steel blade of the knife gleamed silver in the moonlight. Its curved edge dug against Janaan's throat.

"If your friend thinks even of running, it will be your life!" the man warned in a low voice. Yanking Janaan into his chest, he clamped an arm around her waist.

"You!" he ordered, jerking his head at Lauren, "go now to the house."

For an instant she stood unmoving. Adrenaline shot through her as she looked from the man's dark eyes to Janaan's wild ones. Janaan's sharp, raking gasps were the only sound, and in the dim light Lauren saw her friend's mouth part in terror, her whole body go taut as wire.

"Now!"

Her mind reeled with possibilities, all of which flamed and died in a single instant. Looking into the man's hard eyes was like looking straight at death. Lauren might be able to run, but that knife would slash Janaan's throat. He would kill her. He knew it, Janaan knew it, and Lauren knew it. There was nothing she could do but obey.

Light stung her as she stepped into the front room. She heard the door shut behind them.

"Close the curtains!"

Lauren turned to see him tighten his grip on Janaan. "Do it!" he told her.

The cord lay buried in folds of gold velvet. Her fingers felt stiff as she slowly closed the drapes, praying that someone out there would notice, could somehow understand. All she saw through the hazy glass were graves.

"Now take off your clothes."

Lauren froze.

"To your underclothes!"

"Please," she begged. "I can't. . . ."

Long, crooked teeth filled his face with an ugly smile. "I will not touch you!" His voice was low, menacing.

She began to take off her shoes. There had to be something she could do! But there was no phone, no tool to hurt him with, no way to signal anyone, nothing.

"Your shirt! Take it off!"

Lauren pulled the turtleneck over her head, exposing her white lace bra. He smiled and demanded, "Now your pants."

The room was so quiet, so deathly quiet, it seemed the harsh sound of the zipper crashed in her ears. Her jeans dropped to the floor. She stepped out of them and shivered.

With one arm the man pulled a high-backed chair

into the center of the room. The knife danced around Janaan's neck.

"Sit," he commanded Lauren as he gestured toward the chair. On the cold chair she felt so helpless, so exposed. It's a dream, she kept repeating to herself, but she knew it wasn't. It was real. And she was going to die.

The man led Janaan to a wicker chest and rummaged through its contents, then stood with a handful of bright silk scarves.

"Now you tie her," he ordered Janaan, handing her a blood-red scarf. "And if you don't tie enough, I will slit your gut like a pig." The knife moved to an inch from her stomach.

Janaan took the scarf and knelt behind the chair. "Hold back your hands, Laurie," she said in a choked voice.

When Lauren put her hands behind her back, Janaan wrapped the scarf tightly around her wrists. Suddenly Lauren felt cold steel pressed against her throat. The man was standing behind her, one hand caressing her hair as the other slid across her neck.

"Your friend, is she loyal?" He snorted, then looked at Janaan. "Your clothes, also."

Then they were tied together, back to back, with the scarves so tight Lauren felt the blood stop at her wrists. The chairs had been bound to each other with ropes the man tied himself. Satisfied, he stood in front of them. Janaan's panties were silk, Lauren's lace. He fingered each garment at the waist band, grinning as they recoiled, and ran his hands down their bare arms. A gutteral laugh exploded from his mouth.

"You give yourselves a compliment if you think I would touch you spoiled rotten American girls."

He crossed to the couch, sat down, and lit a cigarette.

"So, you know who I am. Do you know what I am called by?"

The chairs stood parallel to the sofa; if Lauren and Janaan turned their heads they could both see him. Neither one of them moved.

"I am called Bokour. You may call me Bokour in your remaining moments."

Smoke curled from his lips. "I remember you, Janaan. Do you remember me also?"

"Yes." Janaan's voice was as cold as his. "What did you do to my brother?"

"Your brother is safe and doing well. A healthy boy. Thirty thousand dollars is what he brought me. You see, it is the beauty of what I do—no one looks for my babies. I harvest them from the ground"—he clenched his hand—"like food from the earth. And no one looks for them. They are mine."

"And Rachael?" Lauren had to know.

"Ah, the little girl. She is fine also. I wait until the babies are taken out of the house, for a walk, for play, to the doctor, and I touch them."

After another drag from his cigarette, he stood and crossed to the bookcase, lifting a silver container from the cluttered shelves.

"In my country, I am a doctor. I make a powerful

medicine, from a simple fish, that will turn you as if dead. In my country, I make the zombie. We take him from the grave, also. But my country is poor, and I think of America, and I think of my poison."

He moved toward a hall closet and opened the door.

"I see the rich people of this country, how they can buy big cars and houses, but they cannot buy the one thing they want most. They cannot buy the baby."

Reaching to the top shelf, he pulled down a metal box.

"I think of these rich Americans, and I think of my poison. And it comes to me. I think of selling the babies. I think of staying in America for a time, to return to my poor country with the power money buys. But, in my plan, I have a problem."

Bokour returned to the couch and carefully opened the box. A large paper rectangle rested on top of its contents. He held it in one hand, ripped it open, and removed a pair of surgical gloves.

"My problem is, in this country, you take the blood. A person dies, and you take the blood." He pulled on one glove, carefully working his fingers into the tips, then the other. "You embalm your dead." Bokour snapped the latex against his wrists and smiled. "And then I know. Three religions do not take the blood. Three religions place the dead quickly in the ground. And I think," he said, tapping his forehead, "I will take from these." A pair of cloth workman's gloves was lifted from the box next, the same gloves he had worn when he touched Rachael.

"You see a perfect plan," he said, turning to look at them. "Crib death, everyone thinks, so they do not investigate. But I did not know you would be there, Janaan. I am careful. I check so the families do not intertwine. You were there, and I did not know. It is a shame."

"What happens if you can't get the babies out?" Janaan demanded. "Some Moslems don't even use caskets!"

Bokour shrugged. "In every business there is risk. I am in America. Here a casket is used. If not?—I do not lose so much."

Lauren's insides turned to water. She pulled against the scarf that bound her, but it held fast.

"What are you going to do? The police will know something's wrong if we're murdered."

"You are right, Janaan. But they will not know. You see the scarves? They will leave no mark. I will give you the same poison I gave the babies."

"We won't tell anyone," Lauren pleaded. "They'll know we didn't die of crib death like the babies. Please don't hurt us!"

"Not crib death!" He laughed. "Such grown girls! No, I will do to you as I did to an enemy of mine. I will take your clothes and fold them carefully by the shore of a pond. Just the way you would. I will put my poison on you, and you will not breathe. My poison does not kill, but you will be unable to move. Then I will throw you into the water, and you will drown. It will seem as though you foolishly went for a swim in the night. It is all so simple, is it not?"

Hot tears rolled down Lauren's face. She was going to die. Right here, in this room. She would die like Rachael, but no one would pull her from the grave.

"Where is my brother?" Janaan asked coldly. "If you're going to kill me, I would at least like to know."

The lid of the silver container scraped eerily as Bokour twisted it open. A plastic bag was folded inside. He very carefully uncurled its edges.

"My poison will pass through the skin. Too much, and you die instantly. The heart will not beat. But the right amount, and the heart will beat only once in five minutes. The breathing is so slow that no one can hear it. I must take the babies from the ground quickly, before the air in the casket is gone. If not, the brains will die."

He walked closer, holding the container in front of him.

"Can't you tell me where Adam is?" Janaan started to shriek. "What difference will it make?"

Bokour's eyes narrowed as he looked at her. Then, shrugging as if it couldn't matter, he said, "Your brother is in New York. I keep his name in a book for when I am done here. I will take my book, and I will mail the rich parents a letter. I will tell them to send money. Their child is in jeopardy, it will be taken from them and returned to the real parents, unless they give me money as I ask. I will be rich until I am very old."

"New York?"

"Yes."

He paused. "One must go first. Which friend will it be?"

"HELP!!!" Lauren screamed. "God, somebody help us!"

"Corpses will not open their graves to help you, and that is all who live here. You will go first."

In front of Lauren, he dipped his finger into a gray powder. Screams choked her throat. Bokour reached his hand toward her. A line of powder lay on his gloved finger. He would touch her, she would die. Every one of her senses seemed as sharp as the blade of Bokour's knife. He had bound her, roped her arms flush against her sides. She was immobile, helpless, except . . . Bokour took one more step. Lauren drew all her strength into her legs, and, as he reached for her, kicked him as high and as hard as she could.

The silver container spun from his hand, whipping through the air. Bokour's eyes widened as the container hit him squarely in the face. A choked scream, like the screech of an owl, then he reeled away from them and clutched his throat. He fell onto the floor, writhing on his back. The gray powder covered his mouth and eyes and shrouded his moist tongue in ash. His eyes rolled to the back of his head. His body jerked in spasms, and then he lay, motionless, at Lauren's feet.

17

The dawn swept pale colors across the sky when Detective Michaelson pounded on the caretaker's door. An all-points bulletin had been issued by midnight, but fruitless hours had dragged by until a black-and-white unit spotted Janaan's car parked beside the cemetery gate. At 5:45 A.M. Officer Tyson discovered Lauren's knit cap caught in the thicket's branches; moments later the men stood at the door.

"Police! Open up!"

"Help us! We're in here! Oh, God, help us!"

The door burst open. Guns cut through the air as the officers whipped around the door frame in attack position. Slowly their arms dropped as they discovered Janaan and Lauren, pale and shivering, bound back to back in the center of the room. Bokour's twisted body lay inches from their feet.

"What the . . . ?" Detective Michaelson put his gun back in his holster and hurried toward them. "Is he the only one here?" he asked as he stepped over Bokour.

"Yes," Janaan said hoarsely.

Michaelson bent over Bokour's body, his hand outstretched toward the silver container on the corpse's face.

"Don't touch that!" Lauren screamed. "It's poison!"

Michaelson's hand recoiled. He looked up at Lauren, then slipped off his plaid jacket and laid it gently across her chest. Tyson pulled at the scarves that bound them, trying in vain to work the knots free.

"Get a knife and cut the damn things off!" Michaelson ordered. "But first give Janaan your coat, Tyson. She looks cold."

The police station wasn't nearly as intimidating as it had been the first time. In the room where they sat now, brown wood panels absorbed the fluorescent lights and cast a warm glow. Two large palm trees splayed the corners with green, and a dried flower arrangement rested sedately in the middle of a walnut conference table.

Janaan swiveled her padded chair toward Lauren. "We've come up in the world, Laurie. You should have seen the toilet they put me in at first!"

"I know, I was just thinking the same thing. The room they put me in was a bilious green hole!" It had been an hour since the detectives found them, and their moods had swung from incredible highs to desperate lows. Right now everything seemed funny. Laughter caught in their throats as Detective Michaelson, Detective Bentner, and a man they didn't know entered the room.

"Hello, Janaan, Lauren," Detective Michaelson greeted them. "This is Dr. Sherwood. He's our medical examiner. I'd like to thank you both for talking with us. I know how hard this whole thing has been on you. But we've got some important questions to ask and I hope you can help us put this whole case to rest."

"I have a few questions myself," Janaan announced, suddenly serious. "Like, did you find the book? Do you know where Adam is?"

The three men sat down. Bentner leaned forward and clasped his hands, resting them on the walnut tabletop.

"We found the ledger. We had fifteen men scour that place, and one of our detectives discovered it about thirty minutes ago, hidden in a hollowed-out book. If Bokour hadn't told you girls it existed, we might never have found it."

Janaan grabbed Lauren's hand under the table and squeezed it. "Do you know where Adam is?" she asked again.

Michaelson and Bentner exchanged glances. Bentner pulled a stick of gum from his pocket, then tapped it nervously against the table.

"Your parents should be the ones to tell you that, Janaan. They're on their way here right now. Your parents, too, Lauren."

"I can't wait! I have to know now!" Janaan pleaded. "Is Adam all right? Is he alive?"

Michaelson ran his hand over his mouth, then leaned forward in his chair. He looked from Lauren to Janaan.

"I know your parents wanted to be the ones to tell

you, but . . . Well, here it is. Yes," he said, "he's alive. We found him. We've got men going there right now. As I understand it, your folks will be leaving for New York in a matter of hours. Congratulations, Janaan. You've got your brother back."

Lauren swung around to hug her friend tightly. She could feel hot tears spill into her hair, and could hear Janaan's choked laughter mixing with sobs. Lauren felt her throat knot.

"And Rachael?" she asked tightly.

"According to the book, she was sold to a couple in Arizona. The Blooms are being notified right now."

Adam and Rachael alive!—and coming home! Resurrected! First a theory, then a dream, now an incredible reality.

Lauren and Janaan held one another until Michaelson cleared his throat and said, "I'm sorry, ladies, but we still need to know more—"

"About the man that did this," Dr. Sherwood broke in gently.

"That's fine, really," Janaan said, wiping her eyes. "I feel great. Except we need some Kleenex. What do you want to know?"

"The poison," Dr. Sherwood began as Michaelson handed them tissues. "Did Bokour ever tell you what kind of fish he made it from?"

"No." Lauren rubbed a Kleenex under her eyes. "Just that it was a fish. And he said in his country he used it to make zombies. He said he was a doctor."

"Oh, he was a doctor, all right. A witch doctor.

That's what his name, Bokour, means," Dr. Sherwood explained. "Before coming to meet with you, I called a colleague of mine. If the test proves to be what he suspects, then Bokour's gray powder is made from the puffer fish. The female's ovaries are so toxic that one touch"—he snapped his fingers—"means instant death. But mixed in the exact amounts, the victim slips into a comalike state, a living death. The heart slows, the respiration all but stops. One man in Haiti was declared dead in an American hospital, buried, and turned up walking the streets five years later. The amazing thing is that the drug fooled an American team of physicians. It's really quite exciting."

"Exciting!" Janaan exploded. "It's horrible!"

Dr. Sherwood colored. "I'm sorry, I was thinking of the medical possibilities, not about what you've been through. You see, surgery could be virtually redefined in the future. If administered correctly, the patient awakens with absolutely no side effects. Imagine brain surgery where there's no problem with blood loss because the heart doesn't beat! Imagine—"

"Excuse me, Doctor, but these girls have been down a rough road," Michaelson broke in. "I'm sure they want to go home and get some rest."

Detective Bentner turned to Janaan. "Just a little bit longer and we'll let you go. Honest! Now you said you remembered seeing Bokour the day Adam died?"

"He was walking down the street when I had Adam in the stroller. He just stopped for a second and chucked him under the chin—you know, that what-a-sweet-baby routine. Did Mrs. Meyer remember seeing him?"

"We showed her a picture from his driver's license. She said she wasn't sure, but she thinks she saw him at the grocery store the day her son died. Same sort of thing, touching him, then moving on. We found a lot of notes in the ledger, and believe me, this man knew everything about these people—he must have been watching their houses for weeks. Then he moved in for the kill and took the bodies—I mean, the babies—at night from the graves. A real ghoul."

"I can't believe he got away with it!" Lauren exclaimed.

"Not just here, but other places, too. The ledger contained names of babies from seven states. He took only the ones he thought he could market easily, which is most likely why he picked blonds. We found some Vermont newspaper want ads in his bedroom with the names of prospective parents circled—Vermont allows couples from all over to advertise for babies. That must have been how he made his contacts."

"A perfect plan, if you have ice in your veins," Bentner cut in. "The thing was, nobody was looking for these babies. Their faces weren't on any milk cartons, nobody put their pictures on light-poles. As far as the rest of the world was concerned, these kids were dead."

Lauren exhaled slowly. "He said he was going to blackmail the people he sold the babies to. He said he'd be rich until he was very old."

They were all quiet until Michaelson said, "Well, he was an evil man, but thank God he recorded every name of every baby he did this to."

"There'll be some happy reunions this summer," Bentner said softly.

Michaelson sat up straight. "I—this entire department—wants to thank you girls. We were thinking with mental blinders on, but you two kept trying all the possibilities. And, Janaan," he said, his eyes sober, "I know I speak for everyone when I say I'm sorry we misjudged you. You, too, Lauren. Your parents should be very proud."

18

Lauren and Janaan stood in front of the airport security rope, a thin yellow cord separating them from the horde of newspeople who clamored behind them. Adam's story had somehow leaked to the press, and a sea of cameras and microphones swelled against the cord like an electronic wave as men and women fought to capture this modern-day resurrection.

They watched in tense silence as the plane taxied the runway, circled, then slowed to a stop. After workers secured a connecting tunnel to the airplane, Lauren and Janaan waited for what seemed an eternity until the first passengers trickled through: two businessmen in dark suits, then a wealthy-looking older woman followed by a girl in a wheelchair. Lauren could feel her tension build as more people streamed into the concourse.

"Where are they?" Janaan asked as she quickly scanned each face. Suddenly she gasped, "Adam!"

Abdul and Nancy Kashad emerged clutching Adam between them, their faces flushed with emotion. Janaan broke free and raced toward them, and they were together, Janaan, her mother, her father, and eleven-month-old Adam, more angelic than Lauren remembered.

"Is it really you? Oh, Adam! Look what I brought you," Janaan sobbed, holding up a trembling hand. Three heart shaped bracelets dangled from her wrist. "See, little guy, I remembered."

Adam's eyes widened as he reached for Janaan. Soft blond hair still curled gently around his face, but it had darkened to a deep honey. His round face and arms had thinned, his nose had lengthened, but when he smiled, he was Adam.

"Welcome home," Janaan whispered. She held him in her arms and kissed his forehead.

Suddenly Lauren felt the crush of Abdul Kashad's strong arms as he enveloped her, his rough cheek pressed against hers. He broke away and held her face between his hands. Those dark eyes, once so frightening, now seemed warm and gentle. In a choked voice he said, "Thank you, Lauren. Thank you for my son."

"I'm happy for you, Mr. Kashad."

Dropping his hands, Abdul Kashad turned back to his family. Lauren stood apart and watched. The cameras clicked and whirred as the reporters began shouting questions.

"Is it true they've located the other two babies?"

It was true, she knew. Rachael was coming home tomorrow.

"How long was Adam buried?"

"How much did the New York family pay for your son?"

As if on cue an army of police officers and security people appeared. They formed a human chain around the Kashads and began to move them forward.

"Where's Laurie?" Janaan cried.

"Right here," Lauren answered, running behind her. "Listen, Janny, you go on. I'll just sneak out to my car."

"No, come with us!"

The noise was deafening as they moved through the reporters. Janaan had grabbed Lauren's arm to pull her into the circle. Lauren shook her head. "This is a time for your family. Your brothers are waiting for Adam at home."

"But I want you to be there, to celebrate with us!"

"I know." She hugged her and said, "I'll see you later."

"Wait! This is for you." Janaan reached into her purse and held out a small square package. "I wanted to give it to you at my house, but . . . just open it."

Lauren tore away the pastel paper and saw antique brass framing a new copy of the picture Janaan had destroyed.

"I stopped at your house yesterday and got the negative. I took it to a fast-photo place—I hope you like it."

"Janaan, we must go now," her father broke in. "The crowd . . ."

"Just a second, I'll be right there." Janaan turned toward Lauren and took her hand. "A long time ago I told you why I ruined it. Now it's fixed. I think you know why."

"Janaan!"

"Coming! I'll call you, Laurie, really soon."

Janny's right, Lauren thought. I do know why. She's whole again. Adam was alive, and in a very real way, Janny's father was alive again, too.

Lauren watched as reporters engulfed the Kashad family. They banded together like an eye in a human storm, then disappeared into a room marked Personnel.

The nightmare was over.

ALANE FERGUSON'S first published story, *That New Pet!,* is a picture book illustrated by Catherine Stock. It shows the author's marvelous sense of humor, and was, in part, written from her experience as the mother of young children. *Show Me the Evidence* is her second book, and her first novel.

Alane Ferguson's interest in writing began when she was ten years old and her mother, the as-yet-unpublished author Gloria Skurzynski, began writing stories and asking for her comments.

The author and her family live in Sandy, Utah.